MOTIVE FOR MURDER

"If the rest of the place looks exactly the same as when you were here previously, and only the mattress appears to have been disturbed, then whomever came here and stole Otis' money knew exactly what he or she was looking for and where to find it," Sergio said.

Hayley walked over and inspected the mutilated mattress.

It made sense.

Sergio moved up behind her. "Who else besides you knew Otis kept his money in there?"

Hayley winced.

Sergio turned Hayley around. "Did Danny know about the money in the mattress?"

Hayley nodded.

She couldn't believe it.

She didn't want to believe it.

Could Danny have killed his own uncle for forty grand?

Books by Lee Hollis

Hayley Powell Mysteries
DEATH OF A KITCHEN DIVA
DEATH OF A COUNTRY FRIED REDNECK
DEATH OF A COUPON CLIPPER
DEATH OF A CHOCOHOLIC
DEATH OF A CHRISTMAS CATERER
DEATH OF A CUPCAKE QUEEN
DEATH OF A BACON HEIRESS
DEATH OF A PUMPKIN CARVER
DEATH OF A LOBSTER LOVER
DEATH OF A COOKBOOK AUTHOR
DEATH OF A WEDDING CAKE BAKER
DEATH OF A BLUEBERRY TART
DEATH OF A WICKED WITCH
DEATH OF AN ITALIAN CHEF
DEATH OF AN ICE CREAM SCOOPER

Collections
EGGNOG MURDER
(with Leslie Meier and Barbara Ross)
YULE LOG MURDER
(with Leslie Meier and Barbara Ross)
HAUNTED HOUSE MURDER
(with Leslie Meier and Barbara Ross)
CHRISTMAS CARD MURDER
(with Leslie Meier and Peggy Ehrhart)
HALLOWEEN PARTY MURDER
(with Leslie Meier and Barbara Ross)

Poppy Harmon Mysteries
POPPY HARMON INVESTIGATES
POPPY HARMON AND THE HUNG JURY
POPPY HARMON AND THE PILLOW TALK KILLER
POPPY HARMON AND THE BACKSTABBING
BACHELOR

Maya & Sandra Mysteries
MURDER AT THE PTA
MURDER AT THE BAKE SALE

Published by Kensington Publishing Corp.

A Hayley Powell
Food & Cocktails Mystery

DEATH OF A PUMPKIN CARVER

LEE HOLLIS

KENSINGTON PUBLISHING CORP.

http://www.kensingtonbooks.com

KENSINGTON BOOKS are published by

Kensington Publishing Corp.
119 West 40th Street
New York, NY 10018

All Kensington Titles, Imprints, and Distributed Lines are available at special quantity discounts for bulk purchases for sales promotions, premiums, fund-raising, and educational or institutional use.

Special book excerpts or customized printings can also be created to fit specific needs. For details, write or phone the office of the Kensington special sales manager: Kensington Publishing Corp., 119 West 40th Street, New York, NY 10018, attn: Special Sales Department, Phone: 1-800-221-2647.

Kensington and the K logo Reg. U.S. Pat & TM Off.

ISBN-13: 978-1-4967-0254-8
ISBN-10: 1-4967-0254-9
First Kensington Mass Market Edition: September 2016

eISBN-13: 978-1-4967-0255-5
eISBN-10: 1-4967-0255-7
First Kensington Electronic Edition: September 2016

10 9 8 7 6 5

Chapter 1

Halloween was Hayley Powell's favorite day of the year, but it was also incredibly dangerous.

Especially for her waistline.

All that candy.

The peanut butter cups.

The candy corn.

The mini Milky Way bars.

Of course, every year without fail, she would stock up on every sweet imaginable. More than all of the trick-or-treaters who showed up at her door could possibly stuff into their orange plastic pumpkins that they hauled around the neighborhood.

No, she was always left with a candy overflow.

So she had always carefully hidden her stash from her two kids when they were younger so she could gorge in peace when they weren't home. Her kids were much older now. One was in college. The other a junior in high school. They weren't so rabidly determined to get their hands on free candy anymore.

But old habits die hard.

And Hayley still found herself hiding candy around the house.

As office manager at the *Island Times* newspaper, it was also her responsibility to have plenty of treats on hand in case any pint-sized ghosts, goblins, witches, or werewolves might come into the office with their parents in search of candy.

She certainly didn't want them leaving disappointed.

So as the office wall clock inched closer to five in the afternoon, which was her usual quitting time, Hayley's eyes never left the ceramic bowl of Gummy Bears that sat within her easy reach. She was always after her kids, even now as young adults, not to indulge in treats before dinner, but those chewy, delectable, oh-so-delicious-looking, lip-smacking Gummy Bears seemed to be calling to her and making her mouth water.

Just try one.

Yeah, right.

One.

When had she ever stopped at just one?

The next thing she knew she was scooping up a fistful, popping them three or four at a time in her mouth, closing her eyes, relishing in the familiar fruity taste and soft jelly bean texture.

"Good night, Hayley," Bruce Linney said as he blew past her from the office bullpen, heading for the door.

Her mouth was full and she was chewing as fast as she could, but there were too many Gummy Bears in her mouth to swallow all at once, and she couldn't speak.

Bruce noticed her nonresponse and stopped at the door. "Everything all right?"

Hayley nodded.

Bruce took one look at the half-empty bowl of Gummy Bears and Hayley's bulging chipmunk cheeks.

It didn't take the cunning deductive skills of Hercule Poirot to solve this one.

"Save some for the kids, okay, Hayley?"

Hayley narrowed her eyes and crinkled her nose, making as mean a face possible given the sad fact she could hardly voice her displeasure at the moment.

Bruce winked at her, smiled, and disappeared into the chilly autumn evening as orange and red leaves from the tree next to the office swirled around him.

Hayley's harsh opinion of crime reporter Bruce Linney had softened during the previous six or seven months. They had worked together on a story for the paper and discovered, much to both their surprise, that they actually didn't despise each other. In fact, they worked rather well together as a team, and even though they still rubbed each other the wrong way on occasion, at least the constant bickering and barrage of insults they had exchanged on a daily basis had quietly subsided.

And besides that, Bruce had also recently started working out at the gym more, trimming a good portion of his belly fat and putting on some serious muscle.

It was impossible not to notice.

Although Hayley always loved a nice bearish man

she could grab onto, there was also an attitude shift in Bruce as he shed his excess weight and felt recharged physically. He seemed more confident, happier, more at peace. Which was a big change from when he was smoking and drinking and barking at Hayley for her irritating penchant for trespassing into his crime-solving territory.

No, the new Bruce was far more palatable.

And dare she say, sexy.

Hayley stuffed another handful of Gummy Bears in her coat pocket for the five-minute ride home.

She promised to prepare a healthy meal for herself and the kids tonight.

Whenever they got home.

She rarely saw them anymore.

Gemma was home from the University of Maine in Orono continuing her work-study program at the office of Dr. Aaron Palmer, Hayley's ex-boyfriend and the town veterinarian. Dustin, an aspiring filmmaker, was off wheeling and dealing, scouting locations and casting his next opus as if the small town of Bar Harbor, Maine, was actually his own personal East Coast version of Hollywood.

As Hayley pulled into her driveway, chewing on her last Gummy Bear, her jaw dropped open and the last bit of the rubbery candy toppled out of her mouth and into her lap.

She couldn't believe her eyes.

Right there on the front porch were two jack-o'-lanterns that had not been there when she left for work that morning.

The kids hadn't been home all day.

She knew that for a fact since she had spoken to both of them less than an hour ago.

One of the pumpkins had been expertly carved into the face of Batman.

The other was a dead-on caricature of Harry Potter.

Batman was Dustin's favorite fictional character from childhood.

Harry Potter was Gemma's.

Hayley felt her heart beating faster, ready to burst out of her chest.

There was only one person in the world who could have left those jack-o'-lanterns on her front porch.

Her ex-husband, Danny.

He used to carve those exact same drawings every year for the kids when they were little.

It was one of the few tasks he could be counted on to complete.

Hayley jumped out of her car and ran to the porch to inspect the pair of jack-o'-lanterns up close.

They were definitely Danny's handiwork.

Which could only mean one thing.

He was sending her a direct message.

Danny was letting her know he was back in town.

Which, in Hayley's mind, was hardly a good thing.

Because whenever Danny Powell showed up, trouble soon followed.

And Hayley had no clue at this point in time just how much trouble was ahead.

Big trouble.

Chapter 2

When Hayley pulled up to the ramshackle cabin tucked in the woods of Tremont on the other side of the island from Bar Harbor, she saw smoke wafting from the chimney. She knew her ex-husband Danny's uncle Otis was home.

And as she stepped out of her car, there was no mistaking the screaming, wailing animal cry of Axl Rose from Guns N' Roses, Danny's favorite band, being blasted from inside.

That was all the proof she needed.

Danny was here and he was probably inside smoking some weed and guzzling down some of his favorite uncle's homemade moonshine.

Two of his favorite pastimes.

Otis was the one who taught Danny how to carve pumpkins when he was a kid. It was the only nice thing he did teach him. The rest of his educational lessons were hot-wiring cars, selling pot, and out-running the police.

Hayley had always been attracted to the "bad boys" when she was growing up.

Until she actually ended up marrying one.

After ten years of marriage to Danny, she was officially cured.

But he wasn't all bad.

He did have a few good points.

He fathered two wonderful children and he loved them to bits.

He worshipped those kids and would do anything for them.

Danny definitely had a soft, gooey center.

He also sported rugged good looks and was a sweet-talking charmer, both of which he maximized to his full advantage.

He would screw up time and time again with one scheme or another, and then when his back was against the wall, he would pour on the charm and flash that high-wattage smile. Hayley, not to mention almost everybody else in town, would fall for it ad nauseam.

Hayley would find herself saying, "I think he's finally maturing" or "This time he's really going to change" and inevitably she would wind up disappointed and heartbroken.

After they divorced and he moved to the Midwest their relationship improved slightly, mostly due to the distance between them, but they would always be a part of each other's lives because of the kids.

Hayley marched up the dirt path to the faded front door and rapped on it with her fist.

There was no answer.

Probably because she could hear Danny and Otis screaming along with the song playing on the sound system. Something about being in the jungle, feeling a serpentine, and wanting to hear someone scream.

Hayley couldn't help but roll her eyes.

Really?

She banged on the door harder.

Still no answer.

She tried the knob.

The door was unlocked.

She swung it open to see Danny and Otis, arms around each other, small jugs of moonshine in their free hands, faces beet red from screeching, swaying back and forth, bobbing their heads up and down, totally caught up in the song.

The blue glass bong with a white skull on the side that sat on the scratched-up, barely erect wooden coffee table in front of them confirmed her suspicions that they would be high on weed as well as drunk when she found them.

Otis looked like he had just flown in from Duck Dynasty Headquarters in West Monroe, Louisiana. He had a sagging, thin, weathered face and a long, reddish beard that reached all the way down to his belly button. He wore an Army-green T-shirt and a red-and-black checkered hunting shirt over it, jeans smudged with caked mud, and a pair of scuffed tan hiking boots. Danny was in a tight-fitting black T-shirt that showed off his muscles, and tight jeans and black boots. It was obvious he still liked to work out. That was another weapon in Danny's arsenal. He had a great body to go with the charismatic personality.

She ignored how good he looked.

It took years of practice but she was finally immune to his charms.

Hayley looked around the ramshackle cabin.

There was junk everywhere.

Fishing equipment stacked against one wall.

Empty jugs Otis used to fill with his moonshine stacked everywhere.

Dirty dishes piled high in the sink.

Boxes of papers and a rickety metal shelf filled with pot paraphernalia.

Otis was a slob and if not a full-blown hoarder, he was very close to getting there.

They hadn't noticed Hayley standing in the doorway.

Danny set his jug down on the floor beside him and lowered his mouth over the opening in the bong to take a hit, and that's when his eyes met Hayley's.

Without missing a beat, he pushed the bong aside, jumped to his feet, and dashed over to her, arms outstretched.

"Babe, what a surprise!"

He grabbed her in a bear hug and tried to plant his lips on her mouth, but she managed to push him away before he kissed her.

"How long have you been standing here?" he asked, grasping her shoulders with his strong hands.

"What are you doing here, Danny?"

"What?"

"I said what are you doing here?"

"What?"

Danny turned to Otis. "Uncle Otis! Turn down the music!"

Otis was still wailing to the Guns N' Roses song with his eyes shut.

"Sorry, he's a little hard of hearing!" Danny said, before sprinting back to the ratty old couch they were sitting on and searching for the remote. It took him almost a minute to rummage through the discarded newspapers and used joints before he found a sticky, ancient remote and hit the volume button.

The music faded and Otis opened his eyes to find out what was going on.

"Look who's here, Uncle Otis!" Danny said with a bright smile.

"Hayley! How have you been?" Otis said, his speech slurred.

"Fine, Otis. And you?"

"I got arthritis in my hand. Hurts like a son of a bitch. And the doctor says I got a fatty liver but what the hell does he know?"

He probably knew an alcoholic when he saw one.

"Can I get you a drink, Hayley? Otis just whipped up one of his best batches of moonshine I've ever tasted," Danny said.

"No, thank you. Why are you in town?"

"I had some time off . . ."

"You've been working?" Hayley asked with a raised eyebrow.

"Yeah, I got a job. Good one too. Night watchman at a warehouse. Pays well. Decent benefits. Everything but dental."

"And they're already letting you take a vacation?"

"I did some double shifts so I could take a week off."

"And you decided to come here?"

Danny tried to step closer, but Hayley kept him at arm's length.

"Yeah. I've been missing the kids. I got to thinking I hadn't been home in a while so I just kind of found myself driving east. Got here last night."

"And the carved pumpkins on my front porch was your way of telling me you're back?"

"Something like that. I didn't want to just show up on your doorstep unannounced if you weren't ready to see me."

"Good call."

"You're looking prettier than ever, Hayley," Danny said with that engaging smile.

How could he have such perfect teeth and not even have dental insurance?

"So you're not here to borrow money?" she asked, arms crossed, suspicious.

Danny's smile slowly disappeared, his eyes were downcast. "No, Hayley. I don't want any money."

His feelings were hurt.

Or was he just trying to convey to her that his feelings were hurt?

He was that good of an actor.

If he had channeled his abundant energy into performing, he could have been the next Ryan Gosling.

With the same rock-hard abs.

Danny couldn't blame her for being suspicious.

She had fallen for this before.

More than once.

"Danny, if you're short on cash, you come to me. I've got plenty," Otis said, marching over to his bed in a sectioned-off corner of the cabin.

Well, a mattress on the floor.

There was no bed frame.

There were sheets that were once white but now covered in stains (from Lord only knew what) balled up on the floor next to it and a couple of flattened pillows strewn across it.

Otis got down on his hands and knees and stuck

his hand through a slit on the side, fished around, and pulled out a wad of cash. He then crawled back up to his feet and noticed Hayley staring at him.

"I don't trust banks. Never did."

He walked over and tried to hand it to Danny, who waved it away. "No, Uncle Otis. I didn't come here to take your money. I don't want it or need it."

Then he turned pointedly and said to Hayley, "And I'm downright insulted that anyone would think the only reason I came here is because I'm broke."

He waited for Hayley to apologize.

But she didn't.

This was a pattern.

He always made a great show of insisting he was not home because he needed something.

And then, after a few days, once he was able to suck you back in again, he would find a subtle way to ask for what he needed.

He was the master of manipulation.

But Hayley was ready for him this time.

Or so she thought.

Chapter 3

Hayley spent the following morning at Mount Desert Island High School judging a baking contest in the Home Economics class that was recently reintroduced into the curriculum because of an overwhelming demand from both male and female students with big dreams of winning *Top Chef*. After crowning a clear winner, a boy from Southwest Harbor whose Pulled Pork Tamales with Corn Salsa, a recipe he learned while traveling with his family to Mexico City, blew all the other entries away, Hayley sped back on Eagle Lake Road in her car, dreading the pile of work waiting for her in her in-box.

When she arrived at the *Island Times* office, there wasn't anybody around.

No reporters filing stories.

No photographers downloading pictures.

No Bruce Linney hovering around her desk waiting to bother her.

She dropped her bag and sat down to check her e-mail when raucous laughter from the conference room in the back bullpen broke the silence.

She could tell from the wheezing and familiar hysterical giggling that it was her boss, Sal Moretti.

Hayley was surprised because Sal rarely laughed. He usually was too busy yelling.

But when he did lose it, it came at you fast and furious like a flash flood.

And someone today had him in stitches.

She walked in the back and opened the door to the conference room to find Sal nearly falling off his chair, tears streaming down his cheeks, shaking his head, unable to control himself. Across from him was Danny, feet up on the table, flashing his megawatt smile, with his hands clasped behind his head, totally relaxed. "I swear on my mother's grave that when I took that Buick for a joyride, I had no idea it belonged to Police Chief Hall! I mean it was his fault! He left the keys right in the ignition when he went into the Big Apple for his doughnut and coffee!"

"I remember that as if it was yesterday!" Sal howled. "You always had balls, Danny. I could never do half the things you used to do!"

"Oh come on, Sal, I always looked up to you, man. You were a rock star! The story of you sending that letter to all the underclassmen telling them school had been extended for two months to make up for snow days is legendary! There were kids showing up for classes until mid-July!"

"Good thing I graduated the day before I sent that letter out, otherwise I would have been expelled!" Sal said, laughing.

"You were the master!"

"Come on, Danny. I may have inspired you, but I just came first. You topped everything I did when you hired that mariachi band to follow the principal around all day serenading him!"

"Oh man, I thought he was going to burst a blood vessel!" Danny shouted as both men erupted in a fit of giggles.

They still hadn't noticed Hayley standing in the doorway.

"Seriously though, Sal, I looked up to you. Maybe if I followed in your footsteps I wouldn't have turned out to be such a screwup."

"Don't beat yourself up, Danny. You did fine. You married a nice girl. You had two awesome kids."

"And look how that turned out," Danny said quietly.

Hayley felt awkward just standing there listening while both men were still unaware of her presence.

She thought about clearing her throat to alert them.

But then she didn't.

"I bounced a few checks and did a little jail time. You actually went to college, got a degree in journalism, and now look at you. Started your own paper, made it number one, and just look at all those fancy awards you got hanging on your walls!"

Danny turned and gestured to the wall of framed certificates and that's when his eye caught Hayley. He jumped out of his chair at the sight of her and raced over, grabbing her in a hug. He tried to plant another kiss on her face, but she managed to dodge it again like the last time and expertly wriggled out of his grasp.

"Danny, what are you doing here?"

"We've been catching up," Sal said. "I haven't

seen Danny since he left town all those years ago. I don't think I've laughed this hard since I don't know when . . ."

"I do. Last week when you saw me slip on an ice patch outside and fall on my fat butt," Hayley said, folding her arms.

"Oh yeah, right," Sal said, guffawing. "You should have seen her, Danny. One minute she's walking like a runway model up the street, next thing you know she's in the air, arms flapping, and then *thud*, right on her fanny! I spilled coffee all over my tie I was shaking so bad!"

"Aw, were you hurt, babe?"

"Just my pride. Well, I'll leave you two alone so you can reminisce about the good old days. . . ."

"Actually, I was hoping you'd be free for lunch?" Danny asked with a hopeful smile.

Bruce suddenly poked his head in the door. "Excuse me, Sal, I just want you to know I'll be filing my column a little late today. I'm still waiting to hear back from a source so I can do a little last-minute fact-checking."

Danny stepped forward, his hand out. "Danny Powell."

Bruce stared at him, a little confused. "I know. It's me, Danny. Bruce."

There was no sign of recognition on Danny's face.

"Bruce?"

"Linney. Bruce Linney."

"Nice to meet you, Bruce."

"We went to high school together. We were in the same class."

"Oh, well, it was a big class."

"Not really. There were only a hundred and forty-three students in our class. One of the smallest ever."

"Sorry, buddy. But I was a waste case back then. Spent most of my senior year outside in the smoking area getting high."

"We were in the same homeroom. I sat across from you for four years."

"Huh. I'm still drawing a blank. My bad."

Hayley wasn't sure if Danny was messing with Bruce or genuinely didn't remember him, but he was definitely succeeding in getting under Bruce's skin.

If she was to guess, this was Danny exerting his manhood and making Bruce feel small.

For what reason was a mystery.

Bruce was no threat to him.

And she found it appalling that he would purposely humiliate him.

Sal couldn't help but snort as he tried not to laugh.

"I have work to do," Bruce said huffily before storming out.

Danny turned and flashed that blinding smile again. "Seems like a nice guy. Now where were we?"

"You were asking Hayley out to lunch," Sal offered, not noticing the glare from Hayley.

"Oh yeah, right," Danny said, turning to face her expectantly.

"I'm sorry, Danny. I've been out of the office all morning and I have a lot of work to do . . ."

"It can wait," Sal said. "How many times does Danny Powell ride back into town? Go! Have fun!"

Hayley shot him a sharp look trying to warn him to stay out of her personal affairs.

As usual Sal ignored it.

"I can hold down the fort while you're gone," Sal said. "Hayley's really the one who runs this place, Danny."

"She's always been good at taking care of everybody. Come on. I got the perfect place in mind," Danny said, winking.

Hayley sighed. "Let me get my bag."

Her ex-husband wasn't even on her radar two days ago.

Now he was back in town carving pumpkins for the kids, traveling down memory lane with her boss, and taking her to lunch.

It sounded innocent enough, but with Danny Powell, there was always a trick or two up his sleeve.

And she had to stay guarded until she could figure out what it was.

Chapter 4

"How come we never came here when we were married?" Hayley asked after swallowing a pan-seared lemon scallop at the Reading Room Restaurant inside the Bar Harbor Inn.

"Because we were poor back then," Danny said, laughing.

"We still are," Hayley reminded him.

Danny shrugged. "I'll give you that. But it's not every day I get to have lunch with you so it's kind of a special occasion."

Hayley took in the sweeping ocean views and romantic setting.

She assumed when Danny invited her to lunch they would split a pizza and a pitcher of beer at the more downscale Geddy's Pub, but clearly Danny had something a little more fancy in mind.

The waitress appeared with their entrees.

A petite filet mignon with Maine lobster tail for Danny and a roasted rack of lamb with rosemary and garlic for Hayley.

She was certain after gorging on a feast like this, she would nod off at her desk before quitting time.

Heavy meals always made her sleepy.

The waitress, Denise, a statuesque blonde in her late thirties who recognized Danny right away from high school but chose to basically ignore Hayley, whom she ran into all the time, leaned in close as she set the plate down in front of him, situating herself so her ample chest was close enough that he could touch it with his nose.

She had been shamelessly flirting with him ever since they had sat down.

Hayley found it amusing.

"Let me know if the steak isn't cooked to your satisfaction," she cooed, batting her eyes.

Danny picked up his knife and cut into the piece of meat.

Red juice oozed out onto the plate.

"Blood red. Just the way I like it."

"I'm happy if you're happy," she said, not quite ready to leave them alone to enjoy their meal in peace.

"My lamb looks delicious," Hayley said.

Denise turned as if noticing Hayley for the first time and smiled politely, realizing she should at least acknowledge Danny's dining companion. "That's nice."

Hayley stifled a laugh.

"Danny, do you remember that time we went out together?" Denise said, turning her back on Hayley again.

"We dated?" Danny asked, genuinely surprised.

"Just once. We went to the movies in Ellsworth and saw *Clueless*," Denise said, covering her disappointment. "Don't you remember? I recently saw the movie again on Netflix. I had no idea how funny it was since we missed most of it when we first saw it."

"Let me guess. You made out in the back row and missed the whole thing?" Hayley said, smirking.

"Well, yes. We were definitely in the back row. But we did a lot more than just make out. Remember, Danny?"

Danny nodded, focusing on his steak, not wanting to discuss the sordid details in front of his ex-wife.

Hayley was actually enjoying this.

She loved watching him squirm with embarrassment.

His checkered past as a conquering lothario was finally coming back to haunt him.

Danny must have worked his way through half the female population of Bar Harbor before he turned twenty-one.

"Anyway, let me know if you need anything," she said flirtatiously, touching his arm. "Anything at all."

"Thanks, darling," Danny said, lowering his voice just enough that it sounded smoky and sexy and had Denise swooning.

For a minute Hayley thought Denise was going to pass out and need smelling salts, but the smitten waitress collected herself and bounced back into the kitchen, swinging her curvaceous hips and jiggling her perfectly round butt, giving Danny a better view than the breathtaking ocean outside the giant bay window in front of them.

"You know, Becky might not be too thrilled to know you're here flirting with old girlfriends while you're here in Bar Harbor," Hayley said, laughing.

"She wasn't a girlfriend. We went out once and I

barely remember it. Besides, what Becky thinks doesn't really matter anymore."

Hayley set her fork down. "Why? What happened?"

"We broke up," Danny said, shrugging.

"You what?" Hayley screeched, catching herself. "Danny, what did you do?"

Danny, who was about to take a big bite of his steak, dropped it back on his plate. "What do you mean, what did *I* do? Why do you assume I did something to drive her away?"

"Oh, I don't know. Your entire history?"

"That's just mean, Hayley," Danny said with a hangdog face and sad eyes.

He was really good at playing the wronged victim when he wanted to garner sympathy.

"I'm sorry. But you two were together for a few years, and she seemed really devoted to you, and so I just assumed that you did something . . . you know . . ."

"You mean you assumed I cheated on her?"

"Well, since you said it—"

"I didn't cheat on Becky!"

"Okay."

"No, I really didn't."

"I said okay."

"You said okay, but that look on your face says you don't believe me."

"Like I said, Danny, you have a history."

They ate in awkward silence for a minute.

Danny angrily clawed at his lobster tail with a tiny fork.

Hayley chewed on a piece of lamb.

Finally, Danny slammed the hard shell of the lobster

tail back down on his plate. "For your information, I was the one who broke it off. Not her! Me!"

Hayley nodded, biting into another piece of lamb, frustrating Danny who was convinced she was just humoring him.

"If you must know . . ."

"I really don't need to know anything," Hayley said.

"I woke up one morning and realized Becky was just too young for me."

That was it.

That was just too much to bear.

Hayley howled with laughter.

"What? What's so funny?"

It took her a few seconds to compose herself.

"Since when has a woman's age ever, ever been an issue with you, Danny? You've been chasing girls half your age for years."

"That's not fair," Danny said, frowning.

"This has nothing to do with fairness. I'm just stating the facts."

"Okay, so what? I like younger women. That doesn't mean my tastes can't change."

Hayley desperately tried to stifle herself. "How, Danny? How have your tastes changed?"

"I've been thinking a lot lately, and maybe it's time I find a more mature woman to grow old with, someone who understands me and has shared similar experiences. Someone like . . ."

His voice trailed off.

She prayed he didn't go there.

She had no desire to rehash their failed marriage.

She just wanted to enjoy her lamb and then get

back to work, back to her life, without Danny and his typical shenanigans.

They ate in silence some more until both their plates were empty except for a meat bone on Hayley's and a hollow lobster shell on Danny's.

Danny cleared his throat.

Hayley stared out the window at the harbor.

"Screwing things up with you was the worst mistake of my life," he said softly, looking at her, trying to make eye contact.

Hayley didn't answer him.

She just kept her eyes fixed on the small islands dotting Frenchman's Bay in the distance.

Danny's words did seem sincere, even sweet, actually, but she definitely wasn't ready to have this conversation.

To be honest, she still just wasn't buying what he had to sell.

She had seen this winsome side of him too many times before.

Hayley flagged down Denise, who was only too happy to rush over to Danny's side again. "Can I show you our dessert menu?"

"No, thank you. I have to get back to work."

"I'll bring your check," she said, disappointed.

Danny already had his wallet out and handed Denise a credit card. "Let me take care of it."

Hayley was floored.

This was definitely a first.

Danny Powell was picking up the check.

They weren't even going dutch.

He was paying the *whole* bill.

It was as if she had just awakened in some kind of alternate reality.

Danny noticed the shocked look on her face.

"Don't look so surprised. I've been saving."

"You mean you actually have your own bank account now?"

"Yes. Both a checking and a savings. How about that?"

"I'm impressed."

"I'm trying to be more responsible. I figure I'd like to get married again someday and I don't want to be that guy I once was. I really am trying to change."

Denise returned with Danny's card and a slip for him to sign.

Danny took the card and glanced at Hayley. "Hey, imagine that. It wasn't declined."

He got a smile out of Hayley and that made him happy.

Denise pulled a pen out of her breast pocket and handed it to him.

He didn't even look up at her as he added the tip and scribbled his name.

She waited a few seconds for some kind of eye contact before giving up and slouching away, defeated.

Hayley glanced at the credit card receipt and giggled.

Danny sat back and sighed. "What's so funny now?"

"She wrote her number on the top of the receipt."

Danny picked up the piece of paper. "So she did. How about that?"

"You're still a hit with the ladies."

Danny crumpled up the receipt in his hand and dropped it on the table.

Another first.

Danny ignoring a woman trying to slip him her phone number.

Maybe he had changed.

Or maybe this was just an act and he was playing this role as "the new, improved, mature Danny Powell" to get something from her.

It was hard to tell.

He opened the door for her like a true gentleman as they left the restaurant, never once eyeballing Denise, who stood by the hostess station, forlorn and crushed by his blatant rejection.

And to his credit, Danny didn't even pretend to forget his wallet and race back to the table to pocket that piece of paper with Denise's number on it.

Maybe he was telling the truth this time.

But she was determined to keep her guard up.

Do not waver.

This was Danny Powell.

And years of hard experience had trained her to be vigilant and alert.

Chapter 5

"Would you relax? I'm not going to get sucked back in by Danny!" Hayley said, parked on a stool at her brother Randy's bar, Drinks Like A Fish. She had met Liddy and Mona for a quick happy hour round of drinks after work, and the conversation quickly steered toward the hot topic of the day.

Danny Powell was back in town.

"We've heard you say those exact words before, Hayley. Right before you announced the two of you were getting back together," Liddy said. "Right, Mona?"

Liddy glanced over at Mona hoping for some support, but she didn't respond. She just sat on her stool, slumped over the bar and chugging down a Bud Light.

Mona clearly had no interest in jumping into this discussion.

"Well, that was before I married the guy and had two kids with him and put up with his crazy antics for the best years of my life. I've come out on the other side. I'm immune to Danny now."

Liddy eyed her warily. "I'm just worried about you, that's all."

"Well you don't have to be. Look, I can see Danny is working hard to impress me and to pretend he's gotten his act together, but sooner or later he is going to slip up and the old Danny Powell will finally show up again."

"I just want you to be careful . . ." Liddy said.

"Oh for the love of lobster, Liddy, would you stop squawking at the poor woman? She said she's got this. Didn't you hear her? Danny's got no power over her anymore!" Mona screamed, guzzling the rest of her beer and slamming the empty bottle down on the bar.

Randy snapped to attention and spun around from the far end of the bar, noticing her bottle was empty.

He zipped over to the cooler and fetched her another.

"Did she just say 'for the love of lobster'?" Liddy asked.

Hayley nodded. "Yes, she did."

"I say whatever comes to my mind," Mona growled.

"As you should," Liddy said, patting her on the back. "Never keep a thought inside your head. It'll get very lonely."

Randy delivered Mona her next beer and she nodded, took a swig, thought about what was just said, and slammed it back down.

"Did she just insult me?" Mona barked at Randy.

"Big time," Randy said before sailing off to the other end of the bar to tend to his other customers.

Liddy spun back around on her stool to face Hayley.

"Look, I believe you, Hayley . . ." Liddy said,

fingering the rim of salt around her half-empty margarita glass and scraping some onto her finger before licking it off with her tongue.

"Thank you," Hayley said, sipping her Jack and Coke.

"I believe you because I know you have come to accept in your mind that Danny is the past and Dr. Aaron is the future," Liddy said with an impish grin.

"Oh God, here we go . . ." Mona moaned.

"*What*?" Hayley yelled loud enough to garner some curious looks from a few grizzled fishermen at the other end of the bar. "What are you talking about?"

"She was going on about this before you got here," Mona sighed. "She thinks you've still got the hots for the boring animal doctor."

"The proper word is 'veterinarian,' Mona, and he's not boring. He's very nice. He's got a good career, and he's still not seeing anyone. He's a wonderful catch."

"Except for one little thing. He broke up with me!" Hayley screamed.

"That's just because you didn't make enough time for him," Liddy said, slapping the bar with her palm to punctuate her point. "If you ask for a second chance, I'm positive he'll grant you one, and you two can finally be back on track."

"Liddy, read my lips . . . It's over! I didn't fight for Aaron when he ended it because I knew in my heart he was right. We're better as friends. I'm done with that chapter of my life. And right now, I'm very happy and content being single and I have absolutely no interest in jumping back into another relationship anytime soon."

She thought she was being definitive and crystal clear about her intentions, but Liddy just nodded, a skeptical look on her face.

The door flew open and Danny ambled in, wearing jeans and an open plaid shirt and a brown leather jacket and boots, looking like some kind of sexy Easy Rider. He ran a hand through his thick, wavy hair and flashed that smile, which caused even Liddy to drop her mouth open.

She whipped around to Hayley. "Oh, he's looking really good."

Danny strutted right up to Liddy and enveloped her in a bear hug, squeezing her head against his rock-hard chest. "I'd recognize that gorgeous face anywhere. You discover some kind of fountain of youth or something, Liddy? Because you haven't aged a bit."

When he let her go, she was blushing and giggling and had no idea how to respond. She just just kept fixing her hair as she struggled to stop the silly noises coming out of her mouth. Not knowing what to do, she finally picked up her margarita glass and sipped on it until it was empty.

When Danny spied Randy reaching to grab Liddy's now-empty margarita glass, he grasped his hand and held it instead of shaking it. "There's my sexy stud brother-in-law. Look at you. Man, I'm just a no-nothing nobody, but I'm telling you, bro, you should have stuck it out as an actor! I swear with your movie-star looks, right now you'd be bigger than that Thor guy . . . what's his name?"

"Chris Hemsworth?"

"Yeah, him," Danny said, not letting Randy's hand go.

"He's like an Australian sex god!" Randy squealed before catching himself, embarrassed by his high-pitched voice.

"He's got nothing on you, in my opinion," Danny said, a seductive smile on his face. He was always good at charming the socks off both women *and* men.

Especially gay men.

He had an easy way about him, and unlike a lot of heterosexual men, Danny was not threatened by his gay brethren.

In fact, he was flattered by their attention.

Which made him all the more desirable to women.

And that's where he made out like a bandit.

"Oh, stop . . ." Randy said, giggling alongside Liddy now.

"Yes, Danny, please stop. You're laying it on a bit thick . . . even for you," Hayley said, rolling her eyes.

"No he's not. I don't mind if he keeps going," Randy said with a big fat grin on his face.

"It's a shame I'm straight and a lousy shot," Danny said, shaking his head, disappointed.

"Why is that?" Randy asked.

"Because if I was gay, I'd probably challenge that Brazilian husband of yours, Sergio, to a duel in order to steal you away for myself."

"Oh . . . wow . . . that's so sweet . . ." Randy stammered, now redder than Liddy, who had finally gotten herself under control.

"I've always said, if I were to flip, you'd be the one, Randy," Danny said, using his flashy smile to maximum effect.

"Okay, Danny, that's enough . . ." Hayley said.

"Drinks all around, Randy. On me!"

Everyone in the bar burst into applause and raised their glasses in Danny's honor.

Hayley's jaw nearly dropped to the floor.

Danny was buying a round of drinks?

For the entire bar?

Another first.

Randy leaned down and whispered in Hayley's ear, "I always wondered why you left him!"

"Seriously? Have you forgotten about the week you had your grand opening of this bar and he stole cash from your register?"

"He paid me back. With interest. Even after I told him he didn't have to."

Hayley couldn't believe Randy was still susceptible to Randy's alluring personality.

He had certainly been around for all the tears and drama and when the kids were little and asking why their daddy was never around.

But Danny just had this way of making people forget his bad side when he cranked up the charisma.

"Mona! I didn't even see you sitting there!"

Danny breezed over and put an arm around Mona, who slowly turned her head and stared up at him.

Danny flinched.

"Mona, you look . . ."

"Cut the crap, Danny. I look exactly the same. Maybe a few more wrinkles on my face. The point is, you can save your breath."

"So what's new?" Danny asked.

"I had my gall bladder removed. That's about it."

"Well, it's good to see you . . ."

"No, it's not. I make you nervous."

Mona made a sudden movement, as if she was going to lunge at Danny, and it caused him to jump back.

"See? You're about to piss your pants."

Danny decided to double down.

He stepped bravely forward and put his arm back around Mona. "You don't scare me, Mona. We've known each other ever since we were kids . . ."

"If you don't remove your arm I'm going to cut it off and use it as fish bait the next time I take my boat out."

Danny quietly complied, removing his arm. He tried to laugh off the awkward moment. "You haven't changed a bit, Mona."

Mona turned and looked him up and down with a dismissive glare. "Neither have you, Danny."

God bless Mona.

Chapter 6

Gemma was busy coaxing a rather reluctant and moody Maine Coon cat into a carrier so his owner could take him home. She didn't see Hayley and Danny enter through the front door into the waiting room of Dr. Palmer's veterinarian office.

"Come on, Ridley, you're all better now. It's time for you to go home and get back to chasing all the squirrels in your neighborhood," she said softly, giving him a gentle shove on the butt until he was all the way inside and she was able to close the door and turn the latch.

Danny watched his daughter, a big, wide grin on his face.

Hayley could tell he was just bursting with pride.

Gemma was a young woman now, in the middle of a work-study program, gaining real-life experience and hoping to one day start her own veterinary practice.

"Thank you, Gemma, I've never had an animal who didn't want to leave the vet's after an overnight stay. You must have some kind of magic touch," a redheaded woman in a fur overcoat said, picking up the carrier.

"Well, we had some time to bond while I was putting on his ointment," Gemma said, laughing.

She bent down and peered into the carrier where the Coon cat stared out at her, meowing. "See what happens when you chase a raccoon and actually catch it? They can get pretty vicious. Do me a favor and stick to the squirrels, okay?"

The redheaded woman laughed and then turned and walked out of the clinic with her cat and carrier, passing Hayley and Danny and giving them a friendly nod.

Gemma brightened at the sight of her mother, not noticing her father standing just behind her. "Did you come to give me a ride home? I just need another five minutes."

"Look at you. All grown up and wearing a lab coat like a real doctor. This is just too much," Danny said, shaking his head, resisting the urge to get emotional at the sight of his mature, professional daughter.

Gemma's eyes widened and her mouth dropped open. "Dad . . . ?"

Danny stepped around Hayley, his arms spread open. "Come give your papa a big hug, darling!"

Gemma darted across the room and fell into her father's arms, squeezing him tight and resting her head on his broad chest. "Dad, I can't believe you're here! Why didn't you tell us you were coming?"

"Wanted to surprise you," Danny said. "I made your mother promise not to say anything until I could greet you in person!"

"How long are you here for?" Gemma asked, still

not believing he was standing here right in front of her.

Hayley was happy Gemma asked that question.

She too wanted to know just how long he was going to stick around.

"I got no set schedule. I'm definitely hoping to spend time with you and Dustin while I'm here."

"Well, yes, I'm working every day but I have nights and weekends off and . . . . Dustin's going to freak when he sees you!"

"Where is he?"

"He's at home hanging out with his friend Spanky. Are you coming over for dinner tonight?"

"Well, I don't want to put your mother out . . ."

Hayley opened her mouth to suggest he take the kids out to dinner and she would stay home, but Gemma never gave her the chance.

"I'll cook. I'm actually getting pretty good. Mom, you don't have to do a thing. Just relax, have some wine, and leave everything to me."

Hayley nodded, biting her lip, not enthused by the prospect of spending an evening at home with Danny and the kids like they did as a family before the divorce.

Dr. Aaron's elderly full-time assistant, Edna, a severe woman whose typical expression was a sour face as if she were constantly sucking on a bitter lemon, walked out from the back of the clinic and took her place behind the reception desk. She wore an unflattering print dress and a gray wool sweater and blew into her cupped hands because she was cold.

Hayley marveled how someone could always look so resoundingly miserable.

Gemma raised her index finger to her parents. "I just need to talk to Dr. Aaron about something before I leave."

She dashed back over to Edna. "Is Dr. Aaron still with the Labrador?"

"Yes. Why?" Edna asked, lowering her glasses to the edge of her pointy nose.

"I just wanted to talk to him before I leave."

"If you have anything to say to the doctor, you speak to me first."

"Oh, okay. I just wanted to run an idea by him."

"What kind of idea?" Edna said, sighing.

It had been clear from day one that Edna was not happy about Gemma working at the practice. She was obviously threatened by her youthful energy and positive attitude and wanted to maintain a general feeling of musty gloom.

"It's silly, really, but it could be fun," Gemma said, plowing ahead, either unaware or willfully ignoring Edna's disapproving stare. "I was thinking since Halloween is right around the corner we could host a pet costume contest. You know, people could come by the office and we'd take pictures and put them up and then they could vote and we would give out a prize, something like free shots or maybe a gift certificate to Petco in Bangor."

"That's a terrible idea," Edna said, her voice slightly rising and cracking.

Hayley bristled.

She didn't appreciate a nasty old woman putting down her daughter.

But she held her tongue.

Gemma was an adult now and needed to handle her own prickly situations.

"I would take care of all the details," Gemma said, not quite ready to give up. "You wouldn't have to do a thing."

"It's already a circus around here. We are out straight all day long. I don't think the doctor would want to add to all the stress. I'm sorry, Gemma, it's just not appropriate."

"Well, I for one think it's a wonderful idea," Danny said, staring down Edna, his eyes boring into her. He looked as if he was trying to resist leaping over the reception desk and strangling her like a rag doll.

"Well, since you don't work here, your opinion doesn't count," Edna said, unperturbed by Danny's borderline threatening manner. She turned to Gemma. "And please don't bring this up again, especially to Dr. Palmer. He's got enough on his plate right now and needs to stay focused."

"I understand," Gemma said, disappointment in her voice.

As if on cue, Aaron sauntered through the door in khaki pants and a blue dress shirt with the sleeves rolled up, carrying a file folder in his hand, which he passed to Edna. "I'm keeping the Labrador overnight just to be safe. Would you call Mrs. Finch and let her know?"

"Certainly, Doctor," Edna said, adding a slight sweetness to her voice.

Danny bounded across the room and grabbed Aaron's hand, pumping it a few times and startling him. "Danny Powell, Aaron. Nice to meet you."

"Hello. . . ." Aaron said, his voice trailing off, trying to place him.

"We have something in common," Danny said.

"What's that?"

"My wife."

"Ex-wife," Hayley chimed in, a bit too quickly.

"Oh, you're *that* Danny . . ." Aaron said, getting it, looking to Hayley who wanted the earth to swallow her up at that moment. The last thing she ever expected or wanted was for her ex-husband and ex-boyfriend to come face to face and compare notes.

"She give you as much trouble as she gave me?" Danny laughed.

"No . . . not at all . . ."

"Kidding. Kidding. We just swung by to pick up our daughter. She doing a good job for you?"

"Excellent," Aaron said with a smile to Gemma. "I'd be lost without her."

Edna cleared her throat just to make it known she was still in the room.

"Yeah, she makes her daddy proud every day. She works really hard and her head is full of creative ideas . . ."

Hayley's heart sank.

She knew what he was going to do.

And there wasn't anything she could do to stop him.

"Like that Halloween pet costume contest. That sure sounds like a winner to me."

Edna sat upright in her chair, seething.

"What's that?" Aaron asked, genuinely intrigued.

"Go on, Gemma. Tell him," Danny said, encouraging her.

"Oh . . . it was nothing . . ." Gemma sputtered, keeping one eye on Edna whose head looked as if it was about to explode.

"Tell me," Aaron said.

"Well, I thought for Halloween we could have

people dress up their pets in costumes and we'd take pictures . . ."

"And then you could hang them up here in the office and people could vote and you would hand out prizes to the winners! Doesn't that sound like a totally awesome idea?" Danny bellowed, slapping Aaron on the back.

"But I know it's really busy around here so it might not be something we want to do . . ." Gemma said, now in full damage control because she knew she would have to work with Edna every day until Christmas and they already had an undeniably frosty relationship.

"I love it. As long as you're in charge and I don't have to do anything," Aaron said.

"No. I'll do it all," Gemma assured him.

"Let Edna know if you need any help," Aaron said. "I have to make a few calls. Nice to meet you, Danny. Hayley . . . you look great."

He let that one linger a few moments before turning and hightailing it back into his office, which connected to the front reception area.

Edna glared at Danny, incensed.

"Something wrong, Edie?"

"It's Edna."

"Right. You look a little flushed, to be perfectly honest, Edna."

She looked around her desk, completely discombobulated.

"The printer is out of toner," Edna said, her voice shaking.

The tension in the air was palpable as she stood up and stormed in the back to the office supply closet.

"Let's go home and eat!" Danny said, hooking an arm around his daughter's shoulders, a self-satisfied smile on his face.

He opened the door for Hayley and Gemma and ushered them out before yelling back, "'Night, Ethel!"

Chapter 7

"What you need is one of those high-quality HD
cameras if you're going to be a serious filmmaker,"
Danny said, sitting on the couch with Dustin, whose
head was still spinning over the fact his father was at
this very moment hanging out in the living room
with him and his best pal, Spanky McFarland.

"I tell Mom that *every* birthday and Christmas!"
Dustin yelled loud enough for Hayley to hear in the
kitchen where she was chopping vegetables while
Gemma prepared a meatloaf to put in the oven.

"Well, your mistake was not asking your dad!"
Danny said, chuckling.

"Really? You mean it?" Dustin asked.

Hayley bit her tongue.

Again.

Danny Powell was always full of big promises,
getting the kids' hopes up, and then, in the end, not
coming through.

She worried he was up to his old tricks and didn't
want to see Dustin getting hurt again.

"Halloween's coming up so you know what that

means. Christmas is just around the corner," Danny said.

"That would be so cool!" Dustin said.

Hayley reached into the refrigerator and pulled out a bottle of beer, popped the cap off, and strolled into the living room and handed it to Danny. She still instinctively knew when he was ready for another.

"Thanks, babe," Danny said with a wink, and then turned his attention back to Dustin. "What kind of film do you want to make, son?"

"I want to adapt Spanky's new horror novel into a film!" Dustin said, excitement building in his voice.

Hayley turned to Spanky, who was sitting on the floor and surreptitiously hoarding candy corns from a bowl Hayley had set out on the coffee table. "I didn't know you were an aspiring writer, Spanky."

Spanky nodded.

He was a shy boy.

Small and wiry.

Picked on a lot by the bigger kids when he was in grade school.

But all that abuse just strengthened his resolve to be better than them, to make something of himself, and Hayley was happy to see he had finally chosen a path in which to accomplish that goal.

She was proud that Dustin had stuck by his childhood pal through all those years of torment when it would have been easier for him to abandon Spanky and join the more popular cliques. But both boys shared a love of comic books and movies and that managed to tighten their bond.

"Horror story, huh? You like scaring the all the pretty girls so they'll scream and grab you to protect them?" Danny asked, chuckling before taking a swig of his beer.

"I guess . . ." Spanky shrugged.

"Spanky's come up with a real spine-chiller," Dustin said, pointing at a manuscript on the floor next to its author. "He's going to be the next Norman Cross!"

Norman Cross was a best-selling horror and suspense writer who lived half the year at his estate on Lower West Street overlooking Frenchman's Bay. The winter and spring months he spent at his Central Park West apartment in New York or at his getaway compound in Key West, Florida. He had built an empire as the Master of Horror rivaling Maine's other famous fright-meister, Stephen King.

"I was up all night reading it. I couldn't put it down. Lots of blood and gore. It's called *The Devil's Honeymoon* and it's about a young newlywed couple named Kurt and Lila who come to Maine for their honeymoon, and everyone is acting really weird, and it turns out that all the residents in the whole town are these creepy murderous disciples of the devil . . ."

"Dustin, don't give it away! If they want to read it, they're going to have to download it from Amazon or Barnes & Noble or buy the hardcover at Sherman's Bookstore!" Spanky said, popping a candy corn in his mouth.

"That's the way to think, Spanky. Be smart. Don't give anything away for free!" Danny said, slamming his beer bottle down.

Hayley had to laugh to herself that Danny was doling out business advice, given the fact he hadn't saved a dime in his life.

But yet again she held her tongue.

"Maybe you can cast me as the honeymooning husband in your movie version, son," Danny said, leaning forward expectantly.

"He said *young*, Dad. A *young* couple."

"Ouch," Danny said, falling back on the couch. "That one stung. I think I need another beer."

"I'll get it," Hayley said, instantly regretting the fact that she was falling right back into the role of dutiful wife.

Danny sprang to his feet. "No, you relax. You don't have to wait on me hand and foot."

He was really making an effort.

Which only managed to raise her suspicions even more.

What was Danny really doing back in Bar Harbor?

What was his game plan?

Danny Powell always had a game plan.

And it usually involved scaring up some money to pay off a gambling debt or to blow on some extravagance he didn't need.

She was certain of one thing.

His real motive for being here would sooner or later come into focus.

It always did.

Island Food & Spirits
by
Hayley Powell

I'm sure most of you have spotted my ex-husband, Danny Powell, who has roared back into town. As many of you already know, it's hard to miss Danny! I've received nonstop reports of Danny sightings at Paradis True Value hardware store, the Shop 'n Save, Jordan's Restaurant, and (no surprise here) Little Anthony's Sports Bar & Pizzeria. He's also made the rounds in other towns on the island like Southwest Harbor and Northeast Harbor, dropping in on old fishing buddies and former high school classmates.

Now that Halloween is upon us, I took some time to look back on my years with Danny, who so enjoys this time of year. Although when it comes to Halloween, he can usually be counted on for more tricks than treats!

In honor of the native son's return

to Bar Harbor, I decided to whip up one of his favorite fall desserts I used to make when we were married—Pumpkin Bread Pudding.

It brought back some nice warm memories and, alas, a few not so nice ones. One in particular stood out in my mind. Just the thought of it drove me to treat myself to a Pumpkin Pie Martini Cocktail to calm myself down a bit as I played back that fateful Halloween night over and over in my mind.

The night in question was some years ago when my kids were still very little. My besties, Mona and Liddy, strong-armed me into taking a night off from taking care of my kids and accompanying them to a Halloween party at Geddy's Pub where they were holding a costume contest. The grand prize was a whole month of free cocktails. Needless to say, half the town, including us, were determined to win!

The three of us dressed up as the Three Musketeers right down to the pantaloons, feathered hats, and swords. But only Mona and I stuck to the original plan. Liddy insisted on swapping out her pants for a tight-fitting toga dress at the last minute, announcing that we should at least have one sexy musketeer since Geddy's had enlisted an all-male judging panel. Mona just

shook her head in disgust as we headed
out the door.

I had left my two kids in their
father's custody and he promised to
take them to the YMCA Halloween
party held every year for all the children in town. Four-year-old Dustin
was over the moon with excitement
because he was a Batman fanatic and I
had bought the last Caped Crusader
costume available in all of Eastern
Maine. Gemma was going as a cat
with cute headband ears, a painted
cat nose, and pipe cleaner whiskers.
Danny's costume of choice was a
Ghostbuster like his favorite actor, Bill
Murray. They all looked adorable as I
ushered them out the door while the
girls and I put the finishing touches on
our own costumes.

The Geddy's Pub Halloween costume competition was fierce that year
mostly because of the coveted grand
prize of free booze! We were having a
raucous time and everybody was danc-
ing and singing along to retro '70s and
'80s tunes. My brother, Randy, and his
boyfriend, Sergio, had won the contest
with their tribute to the '80s cop show
Miami Vice and their pastel Crockett
and Tubbs outfits.

While I was rocking out to Cyndi
Lauper's "*Girls Just Want to Have Fun*,"
I felt a tugging on my pantaloons. I

looked down to see Dustin in his Batman costume waving up at me.

"Hi, Mommy!"

I was shocked to see him in Geddy's Pub.

"Dustin, what are you doing here?"

I looked around for his father but he was nowhere in sight.

"Dustin, where's your father? How did you get here?"

He pointed over to the bar where I saw Homer and Marge Simpson. Well, actually it was Ted and Carol Jenkins, a nice local couple who were dressed as Homer and Marge Simpson. Their son Timmy was in Dustin's preschool class and he too was a Batman fanatic. They stood there, stone-faced and fuming.

I suddenly put two and two together and my heart sank.

Danny Powell had taken the wrong child home from the YMCA Halloween kids' party.

Ted Jenkins marched over and explained to me that they found Dustin wandering around the YMCA looking for his dad while their own son was nowhere to be found. Luckily, Dustin remembered where his mother would be tonight. Carol just glared at me, her eyes full of judgment. I was fairly certain I would not be getting her vote for this year's PTA Mother of the Year Award.

I grabbed Dustin by the hand and dragged him out of the pub with Carol and Ted Jenkins hot on my heels and Liddy and Mona bringing up the rear. We jumped into two cars and raced over to my house on Glen Mary Road. I muttered under my breath the whole ride, "I'm going to kill him! I'm going to kill him!"

The cars screeched to a halt and we all piled out and ran into the house. Five crazed adults pushed and shoved and yelled all at once while we all tried to slam through my kitchen doorway at the same time. Dustin got down on his hands and knees and just crawled through our legs.

The commotion startled Danny, who stood motionless in the kitchen watching a mob of people pushing their way inside. He dropped the plate of cookies he was holding and Dustin crawled over to grab one and stuff it into his mouth. Danny was flanked by a wide-eyed little girl dressed as a cat and by a tiny Batman.

We were all screaming at once until Mona shoved her way through the crowd and let out a loud whistle that would have stopped a freight train.

Everyone fell silent.

I marched up to Danny and asked,

"Have you perhaps noticed anything out of the ordinary?"

"No. Why?"

And with a flourish, I whipped off the Batman mask to reveal Timmy Jenkins, who was clutching Danny's pant leg, frightened over all the crazy adults waving their arms and yelling nonsense.

Danny's mouth dropped open. I almost felt a bit sorry for him when I saw the light dawn in his eyes and he realized what had happened.

But not enough to let him off the hook.

I berated him for a full three minutes before I heard Mona chuckling, followed by Liddy, and then we were all laughing at the absurdity of the situation.

Everyone but Ted and Carol Jenkins. They failed to see the humor at all. They scooped up little Timmy and charged out of the house, slamming the door so hard the windows rattled.

Danny joined in, howling, until I reminded him that we would be discussing his irresponsibility after the kids went to bed. He bowed his head and slinked out of the room. Luckily, Dustin survived this little drama. We didn't see much of the Jenkins family after that. I overheard someone say at the Shop 'n Save they had moved to the big city of Boston where it was safer and more civilized.

Oh well.

Of course, taking a trip down memory lane always works up a hearty appetite. So thankfully I had my bread pudding fresh out of the oven, not to mention a delicious, soothing cocktail to wash it down with, so bottoms up, everybody!

Pumpkin Bread Pudding

Ingredients
6 cups cubed stale French bread
1 cup heavy cream
1 cup milk
3 eggs
1 16-ounce can pumpkin puree
1 cup brown sugar
1 teaspoon ground cinnamon
2 teaspoons vanilla
¼ teaspoon salt
½ cup raisins

Preheat your oven to 350 degrees. In a large bowl mix your bread cubes with the milk and cream and set aside to let the bread absorb the milk mixture.

In another bowl beat your eggs then blend in the pumpkin puree, brown sugar, cinnamon, vanilla, and salt.

Pour the pumpkin mixture and raisins over the bread mixture and gently combine by stirring.

Pour into a greased 13x9 baking pan and bake one hour or until pudding is firm when a butter knife comes out clean and top is golden brown.

Remove and let cool 30 minutes. Get out some bowls, scoop some in, and enjoy.

Pumpkin Pie Martini

Ingredients
2 ounces RumChata cream liqueur
1 ounce vanilla vodka
1 ounce pumpkin liqueur
Pinch of ground cinnamon for garnish

Pour all of your liquid ingredients into an ice-filled cocktail shaker and shake well.

Strain into a chilled martini glass and sprinkle a pinch of cinnamon on top if desired.

Chapter 8

Hayley was annoyed by the fact that when she went online to research Halloween costumes for women all the descriptions included the words "sexy" or "sultry."

The men's costumes glaringly did not.

Sexy nurse.

Sultry Egyptian goddess.

Sexy police officer.

Sultry dreamy genie.

It was insulting.

But she didn't have time to spend ranting on her soapbox because she had to come up with an idea and fast.

Her solution was simple.

Princess Leia.

Not sexy Princess Leia.

Just Princess Leia.

She had a white floor-length dress and a belt that she could tie around it.

She had a pair of white boots from Disco Night at the Masonic Hall last summer.

She had a wig she could fashion with side buns.

And Dustin had a plastic ray gun in his toy collection she could borrow.

Done.

Problem solved.

She wasn't enthusiastic about going to Mary Leighton's annual pre-Halloween party that night. She just wanted to stay home and watch TV, but Liddy was adamant that she get out of the house and go and just enjoy herself.

And to insure that Hayley didn't try to back out with some lame excuse, Liddy and her boyfriend, local attorney Sonny Rivers, who was roughly half Liddy's age although she would never admit it, showed up to escort her.

Hayley hated the idea of being a third wheel, but Liddy was simply not taking no for an answer.

When she descended the stairs in her Princess Leia costume, Liddy and Sonny applauded warmly.

"See! I knew you'd come up with something great!" Liddy said.

Hayley did a double take.

Liddy was virtually unrecognizable in a strapless minidress with a sweetheart neckline corset top and a gold overskirt with lace trim and panniers and hoops that gave the dress the classic baroque look of full exaggerated hips. Her legs were covered with suggestive white lace thigh highs and she also wore a sky-high powdered white wig and carried an elegant feathered eye mask.

Liddy had obviously embraced the whole "Sexy Marie Antoinette" costume.

It was a getup fit for a queen.

Sonny's costume was almost as impressive. He was dressed as a pirate in a revealing black lace-up shirt that accentuated his smooth barrel chest, a black pirate captain hat, eye patch, billowy black pants, leather boots, and a deluxe seventeen-inch pirate cutlass.

"You two look fantastic!" Hayley said, feeling as if her last-minute thrown-together Princess Leia costume was uninspired.

"I know! I've been searching for the perfect costume for months! Ever since I saw that Sofia Coppola movie about Marie Antoinette on Netflix I've been dying to get just the right look," Liddy said. "And when Sonny showed up at my door dressed as a pirate I nearly fainted."

"Her favorite sex fantasy is being captured by a pirate so I already had everything in my closet," Sonny said.

"Not in front of the child, Sonny!"

Dustin, who was lounging on the couch with Leroy and Blueberry sleeping next to him while watching a Vin Diesel movie, suddenly realized and burst out laughing. "Me! She's talking about me!"

"He's almost sixteen, Liddy, I think he can handle it," Hayley said.

"Doesn't your mother look great, Dustin?" Liddy asked, trying to get Hayley excited about going to the party.

"I like the ray gun," he said giving her a quick once-over before turning his attention back to his movie.

"That's because it's his," Hayley said to Liddy and

Sonny before turning back to Dustin. "Don't give Leroy and Blueberry any more snacks. They're getting too fat. Have a good night. I'll be home early."

"Not if we have anything to say about it," Liddy said. "You need to get your mind off you know who."

"Who?" Hayley asked.

"Dad," Dustin said, petting the top of Leroy's head absentmindedly. "She's talking about Dad."

"Where is he tonight anyway?" Hayley asked, disappointed he was in Bar Harbor and not spending every free moment with his kids.

"He said he had plans. We're going to get together tomorrow night. Bye. Have fun," Dustin said, not taking his eyes off the TV.

After leaving the house, it took ten minutes for Liddy to climb in the back of Sonny's Mercedes parked out front because of her giant, unwieldy, powdered white wig. She had to crank her head to the side in order to keep it firmly in place and not crush the top of it on the interior roof of the car. Hayley jumped in the passenger's seat and Sonny drove them to Mary Leighton's house on Bowles Avenue just a few minutes away.

The party was in full swing when they arrived. A lot of guests had similar ideas. There was an abundance of Avengers and Justice League superheroes and scores of Disney characters that never seemed to go out of style. The hostess, Mary Leighton, was dressed as Maleficent complete with black horns on top of her head and over-the-top white makeup and ruby red lipstick. Music blared and half a dozen people had cleared the middle of the living room to dance to one of Taylor Swift's hit songs while the rest of the costumed guests had to shout in order to carry on conversations.

"I'll get us some drinks," Sonny said, making a beeline for the table with a large punch bowl and stacks of plastic cups.

Hayley and Liddy took in the spectacle before a loud grunting noise caused them to both spin around and find themselves face to face with a prehistoric caveman. His long-haired wig was matted and tangled. He wore a fur pelt over his tall, muscled frame and he carried a big plastic club right out of the Flintstones.

It took Hayley a few seconds before she even recognized him.

"Aaron?"

Aaron snarled and growled some more.

Liddy giggled coquettishly. "Aaron, you look so sexy as a caveman. So manly and powerful."

"I thought pirates were your sexual fantasy," Hayley said with a smile.

"What? I have to be limited to just one?"

Aaron playfully bopped Hayley over the head with his plastic club. "Me drag you back to my cave now."

Hayley laughed.

Liddy fanned herself with her feathered eye mask. "Oh my . . . Is it me or is it suddenly very hot in here?"

"No, it's you. Definitely *you*," Hayley said.

Aaron noticed someone over by the front door. "Excuse me. I just saw a friend of mine come in. I'll catch up with you later."

He touched Hayley on the arm and then weaved

his way through the crowd. Liddy whipped her head around to see who he was so anxious to talk to but shrugged it off when Aaron shook the hand of a golfing buddy who had just arrived dressed as a vampire.

"I heard he just started seeing someone," Liddy said, frowning.

"Aaron? That's nice."

"It doesn't bother you?"

"We broke up months ago. No, it doesn't bother me at all. In fact, I'm happy for him."

"Are you sure you're not just putting on a brave face?"

"No, Liddy. I'm not."

"Aren't you the least bit curious to know who it is?"

"Not really."

"So if I happened to know the name of this new woman in Aaron's life, you wouldn't want me to tell you? I mean it's just a name I've heard in passing. I have no proof they're actually dating . . ."

"No, I don't want you to tell me."

Liddy raised her eyebrow, unconvinced.

"I'm serious, Liddy."

"Okay. I believe you. You'd rather not know."

"Why? Do you know?"

Liddy grinned. "I knew you would want to know."

"I don't. Forget it. It's none of my business."

Liddy suddenly gasped.

"What?"

"Turn around."

Hayley turned her head to see Darth Vader breathing down her neck behind her.

It was a very elaborate costume complete with a black cape and light saber.

"I think he's come to kidnap Princess Leia and whisk her back to his ship to have his way with her," Liddy said breathlessly.

"That's just what *she's* hoping will happen. There's a lot going on inside her head tonight," Hayley said.

"Dance with me," Darth Vader said in a deep, distorted voice very similar to the actual movie character.

He placed his black-gloved hand on the small of her back and led her out to the dance floor where they jumped around for the remainder of the Taylor Swift song before it segued into an Adele ballad and Darth Vader pulled her close to him.

She indulged him for a few moments before her curiosity got the best of her.

"Okay, who are you?"

"Darth Vader," he said, again with the strikingly real *Star Wars* villain voice.

Hayley reached over and yanked up the mask.

"Danny?"

"Hey, babe," Danny said, flashing that charming smile, his expressive green eyes twinkling.

"Did Dustin tell you I was coming to the party dressed as Princess Leia?" she demanded to know.

"No. I swear. It's a complete coincidence. Great minds, you know? What do you think the universe is trying to tell us?"

"It's telling me I need a drink and you're an evil space villain bent on destroying the world," she said pulling away from him and racing over to Sonny who was holding her plastic cup of punch, leaving Danny on the dance floor as a woman in a racy raccoon costume swooped in to take her place and tried to get Darth Vader to dance with her.

Chapter 9

Hayley silently cursed Liddy for drinking too much Bloody Vampire punch, which consisted of rum, orange juice, pomegranate juice, lime, and seltzer and having to be driven home early by Sonny from the party.

They completely forgot about Hayley and abandoned her.

She was about to call a cab when Darth Vader swooped in and offered her a ride home in his rental car.

Hayley tried to politely decline, but Danny was insistent, and now she found herself in the awkward situation of sitting in her driveway next to Danny whose puppy dog eyes seemed to be begging for a good-night kiss.

"Thanks for the ride, Danny," Hayley said, quickly reaching for the door handle.

"It's early. Why don't I come in and say hi to the kids?"

He was angling for an excuse to get his foot in the door.

And she wasn't in the mood to give it to him.

"No. I don't think so. Call them tomorrow and make arrangements to take them out to dinner or something. I'm sure they'd like that."

"Five minutes. Just a quick beer and then I'm gone. I promise."

"You aren't going to give up, are you?"

He pulled down the mask that rested on top of his head and in his best distorted evil voice said, "You underestimate the power of the dark side."

"Why do you say that?"

He lifted the mask again and said with a grin, "I'm quoting Darth Vader. He said that in one of the *Star Wars* movies. I forget which one."

Hayley sighed. "Good night, Danny."

She opened the passenger's side door and slid out. He leaned over to say something but she didn't give him a chance and slammed the door shut.

She hurried up the steps onto the front porch and inside the house. Once inside, she turned back around and watched him sitting there, a frustrated look on his face.

Then he shifted the car into drive and roared away.

Hayley walked into the kitchen to find Gemma in gray sweats and a powder blue T-shirt that read "Keep Calm and Carry On" leaning against the kitchen counter twirling some buttered spaghetti around on a fork and stuffing it into her mouth, a morose look on her face.

"Everything okay?"

She looked up and cracked a slight smile. Her eyes were bloodshot as if she had been crying. "Princess Leia. Nice. You look a lot like Carrie Fisher."

"Now or back when she did the first *Star Wars* movie? And be careful with your answer. I'm helping you pay for college."

"You look good, Mom," Gemma said before sadly going back to focusing on twirling more strands of spaghetti around her metal fork.

"What's wrong, Gemma?"

"I just had a really bad day at work."

"Why? What happened?"

"It's Edna. I think she's trying to sabotage me."

"Why would she do that?"

"To get me fired."

"Well, that's not going to happen. Aaron's told me on a number of occasions how well you are doing."

"I *was* doing well. But then today we got backed up because I supposedly double-booked appointments and it was a complete mess. People were yelling about their sick animals having to wait so long and Dr. Aaron got really stressed and after lunch he checked the computer and my name was typed in the system as the one who scheduled all the appointments."

"So you made a mistake. He'll get over it."

"But I didn't make a mistake. At least I don't think I did. I don't remember booking any of those appointments. I think Edna did and just typed my name next to all of them so Aaron would think it was me. He was really ticked off and didn't speak to me all afternoon."

"Well, did you explain to him that you hadn't done it?"

"I wanted to, but Edna was sitting right there the whole time and she is the only other person with access to the computer so if I said anything it was going to look like I was accusing her and what if I was wrong? I mean, maybe I wasn't thinking one day and forgot."

"You've always been very detail-oriented, Gemma. I can't believe you would do something like that and not remember."

"I know. I thought the whole thing would just blow over, but then at the end of the day Edna and I got into an argument over the Halloween pet costume contest. You know my original idea was to take pictures of all the animals in their getups and post them on the wall so when people came into the office they could vote for their favorite. But Edna said it would make the reception area look too cluttered and refused to allow me to hang any of them. She told me to just post the pictures on our Facebook page, and I explained how half our customers aren't even on Facebook and that it would only be temporary, and I promised to take all the photos down the day after Halloween, but she refused to budge and it got really tense and that's when Dr. Aaron came out of his office and saw us bickering and he wanted to know why."

"Well, I was there when you told Aaron your idea. You specifically mentioned hanging the photos on the wall."

"Right! I thought he would side with me. But he was already mad about the scheduling snafu and he just started yelling that he didn't have time for this, he was late for a Halloween party. He was irritated because I had told him he wouldn't have to deal with any of this and that it was my job to handle all the details like I said I would, and if I couldn't I should just cancel the whole thing. And then he stormed out. It was awful," Gemma said, choking up.

She wiped a tear off her cheek.

"He's just under a lot of pressure. Don't take it personally," Hayley said, gently rubbing her back. "And don't give Edna the satisfaction of canceling the contest. It's a wonderful idea."

Gemma shook her head. "You should have seen Edna's face after he left. She had this self-satisfied smirk that was so obnoxious I just wanted to slap it off her!"

"Well, it's probably best that you refrained from violence," Hayley said, picturing herself hauling back and punching that miserable old coot Edna right in the nose herself. "Just keep your head down and continue doing the best job you know how to do. And if Edna causes you more problems, then talk to Aaron. He's a very reasonable and fair man. It'll work itself out. Follow the advice on your T-shirt."

Gemma looked down at the words.

"Keep Calm and Carry On."

She smiled and then pushed the plate of buttered spaghetti toward her mother.

"I made too much as always. Why don't you get a fork and help me finish it?"

"I thought you'd never ask. Mary Leighton can't make a decent appetizer to save her life. I almost cracked a tooth on her overcooked chicken taquitos."

Hayley crossed to the drawer to grab a fork.

She knew in her heart she was right.

Aaron was fair and decent-minded.

But there was a lingering thought in the back of her mind that perhaps Aaron was being tough on Gemma because of her.

He was technically the one who had ended their relationship.

However, on some level she had made it very easy for him and perhaps things were not as amicable between them as she had initially believed.

No.

He would never take out any anger on her daughter, who only wanted to work hard and do a good job for him and make both him and her mother proud.

He was better than that.

Edna was another story.

And Hayley was prepared to do battle if that nasty, bitter old shrew insisted on targeting her daughter.

In her mind, Hayley knew that Gemma was a smart, intuitive young woman completely capable of taking care of herself and no longer needed help from her doting mother.

But in her heart, Hayley was still the protective mama bear ready to maul any threat that endangered her precious cub.

Chapter 10

"Remember our first date? It was right here at the Criterion," Danny said, looking around the historic Bar Harbor movie theater with its grand chandelier, art deco walls, and musty seats.

"We were juniors in high school, I think," Hayley said, nodding.

"It was around Halloween, too," Danny said. "I brought you to see a revival of *Halloween* because I knew it would scare the bejesus out of you and you'd cling to me through the whole movie. As I recall, it worked like a charm. Just like I told that Spanky kid his story will do."

The 1978 Jamie Lee Curtis slasher classic about a babysitter and her friends targeted by a masked maniac named Michael Myers was one of the scariest movies Hayley had ever seen even to this day. That revival which marked their first date was over twenty years ago.

Hayley remembered how excited she was when popular big man on campus Danny Powell had asked her out on a date. She knew he had a roving eye and any kind of relationship with him was doomed from the start, but she jumped at the chance to go out with him.

They only had the one date.

Danny was the kind of guy who was easily distracted by any shiny object and that object was in the body of Beth Sanford, a pretty, stacked blonde and captain of the varsity cheerleading squad.

It wasn't until several years later when Hayley was working in a local ice cream shop one summer that they ran into each other and things finally got serious. Danny came in for two scoops of blueberry ice cream in a waffle cone and flirted shamelessly with Hayley. He asked her to meet him for a drink after her shift at the Blue Oyster, a local watering hole that was eventually bought by Randy and renamed Drinks Like A Fish. After hooking up that night, the two were inseparable for that whole summer and they were engaged by Halloween.

Hayley wasn't sure she had made the right decision coming to the movies with Danny and the kids.

She was already wary of his intentions and a "family" night certainly didn't accomplish her goal of keeping a safe distance.

But Danny was insistent.

His uncle Otis had a secret moonshine run to one of his high-profile clients and wasn't going to be back until late, and Danny didn't want to be stuck in his cabin in Tremont watching TV and drinking beer alone.

So he was determined to have a fun night out with his ex-wife and kids.

Of course he picked Gemma and Dustin's favorite pizza joint, Napoli, splurging on two large pies, and at one point he had everyone laughing so hard over one of his wild stories from his high school days that Hayley had to catch herself because she felt herself starting to let go and enjoy his company like old times.

She couldn't risk that.

She still didn't trust him.

The lights on the chandelier dimmed and the theater was plunged into darkness as the velvet curtains opened and the coming attractions reel lit up the big wide screen.

Danny casually yawned and stretched his arm out slowly, bringing it down behind Hayley, and shifting his body weight so he was leaning into her.

For a brief moment, Hayley was going to let the move slide.

The seats were small and Danny was a big guy and needed room to stretch, but then as his hand snaked around her left forearm she turned and said, "Danny, please remove your arm."

He stared at her for a second and then cracked a smile. "Sure, babe."

He lifted his arm, respecting her wishes.

Gemma and Dustin made their way through the aisle with bags of popcorn and cups of soda and a whole cardboard tray loaded with boxes of Junior Mints, M&Ms, and packages of Red Vines.

"Are you planning to feed everyone in the theater?" Hayley whispered, stunned by the amount of food they were carrying.

"We're hungry," Gemma said, tearing open the plastic packaging and taking a bite of licorice.

"It's not like we didn't just polish off two whole

pizzas across the street," Hayley said, shaking her head.

Dustin was stuffing fistfuls of popcorn into his face.

"I almost forgot, Dad. Here's your change," Gemma said, reaching into her pants pocket and pulling out a ten-dollar bill and some coins.

"You can keep it as long as you split it with your brother," Danny said, winking at her.

Hayley nearly fainted.

Danny had given the kids forty bucks.

Where was all this spare cash coming from?

He was obviously making a point.

He wanted to make it clear he was a good father.

Generous.

Giving.

Reliable.

Many of the things he hadn't been when they were married.

The previews concluded and the feature film started.

The familiar piano theme from *The Exorcist* began playing and the credits rolled. Hayley loved this time of year when the Criterion Theatre featured a Halloween Chiller series of classic horror films. Unlike *Halloween*, this movie didn't scare Hayley much. She wasn't afraid of the supernatural, only real-life threats like crazed serial killers and man-eating sharks. But she loved the movie anyway and couldn't wait for the part where the little girl possessed by the devil spins her head all the way around and vomits pea soup.

The kids had never seen the film and she was

confident they were going to think the gross-out scenes were cool.

Dustin leaned over Gemma to talk to Danny. "Hey, Dad, when we were standing in the popcorn line . . ."

"Shut up! The movie's started!" Gemma hissed.

She hated people talking during a movie.

It was one of her biggest pet peeves.

"You shut up! You're not the boss of me," Dustin snarled.

"Mom, tell him to be quiet," Gemma whined.

"I was just going to tell Dad about running into two of his friends," Dustin said before turning his attention back to the screen where Max von Sydow was discovering a strange amulet on an archeological dig in Iraq.

Danny swallowed a handful of popcorn and then turned to Dustin. "Who was it?"

Dustin shrugged. "They didn't tell me their names. I asked if they went to high school with you but they said no. They weren't from around here."

Gemma sighed and huffed and rolled her eyes, trying to watch the movie.

Danny whipped his head around and scanned the theater. Suddenly he audibly gasped and his face turned a ghostly white.

He turned back around and stared at the screen, obviously disturbed.

"Is everything all right?" Hayley asked.

Danny nodded, his eyes darting back and forth.

"What is it?"

Hayley spun around and spotted two large muscular men, one bald and goateed and the other with a thick head of wavy black hair and a tan complexion, possibly Hispanic. They sat in the back row and seemed to be staring daggers at Danny.

"Come on. Let's go home," Danny said.

"What? The movie just started!" Gemma whispered.

"I'm not feeling well. You can stay if you want to but I have to get out of here," Danny said, jumping to his feet and dumping his bag of popcorn on the floor.

Danny quickly made his way through the row of seats toward the aisle, knocking knees and stomping on feet and causing a loud commotion.

Gemma and Dustin exchanged confused looks, then picked up the tray of candy, grabbed their sodas, and followed their father.

Hayley couldn't believe what was happening.

But she wasn't about to stay and watch the movie alone.

She stood up and quietly apologized to the patrons as she scuttled past them and chased her ex-husband and kids up the aisle and out a side exit door.

Danny was already halfway to his rental car when Hayley and the kids caught up with him.

"Who are they?" Hayley asked, curious to know why Danny was suddenly experiencing a full-on freak-out.

"Nobody. The pepperoni on the pizza just didn't agree with me. You could have stayed for the rest of the movie," Danny said, inserting the key into the ignition and starting the car even before Hayley and the kids had a chance to jump in.

"What kind of trouble are you in, Danny?" Hayley asked, her tone measured.

"No trouble. Let's go home. We can watch another movie on Netflix."

"We didn't even get to the part of the movie everybody talks about where the devil takes over the little girl's body," Gemma said, pouting as she got into the backseat. "I heard that part was sick!"

"The priests manage to get the demon out of her in the end and she lives happily ever after at least until the sequel which sucked big time," Danny said.

They drove the rest of the way home in silence.

Chapter 11

Hayley huffed and puffed as she tried keeping up with her daughter, Gemma, while they hiked the back road behind the Kebo Valley golf course. It was a dark and dreary Saturday morning, foggy, cold, and drizzling rain. But Hayley was determined to drag herself out of bed, pull on her sweats, and get out the door because she was in desperate need of some exercise after gorging on pizza for dinner and staying up late polishing off all the popcorn and candy they had brought home from the Criterion Theatre while watching *Rosemary's Baby*, a thriller starring Mia Farrow as a young New York City wife whose actor-husband makes a deal with a satanic cult to bolster his career in exchange for impregnating his wife with the devil's spawn.

The plot sounded ridiculous to the kids but they were jumping and screaming by the second hour.

Hayley had dragged along Leroy on their morning walk because he too was in need of some physical exercise. He was not exactly happy to be out in the rain trotting alongside her while she pulled him along by his leash.

"I dread going in to work today," Gemma groaned as she picked up the pace.

Hayley had to break into a run to catch up to her. "Because it's Saturday?"

"No, because of you know who."

"Has Edna done anything else besides the scheduling mishap?"

"Not yet. But it's like she's lying in wait, biding her time, waiting for the perfect moment to strike again and make me look bad. I can't stand the uncertainty and suspense."

"Well, you should really talk to Aaron about it."

"I think that's what she wants. If I go and complain she'll just deny it and it will make me look like a crybaby."

Hayley spotted a black BMW racing toward them, the car's high beams cutting through the thick fog.

"That looks like Liddy's car," Hayley remarked as it sped along the road.

Suddenly as it got closer, the BMW without warning swerved to the left, careening right for them.

"Mom, look out!"

Gemma pushed Hayley hard and she fell into a muddy ditch, yanking Leroy off his feet as his collar choked him and he let out a tiny yelp. Gemma dove after them to avoid getting slammed by the car, which screeched to a stop, pebbles and gravel on the road flying everywhere.

Gemma helped her mother get back up on her feet. Hayley's sweatpants were covered in mud as was Leroy's entire body.

The window on the driver's side slid down, and

Liddy popped her head out. "Where the hell have you been?"

"Good Lord, Liddy, you nearly ran us down!"

"I did not! Why are you covered in mud?"

"Didn't you see us?" Gemma asked, picking up Leroy and petting his muddy head to calm him down.

"Yes. Why do you think I stopped? I've been looking all over for you! Why haven't you returned the four voice mail messages I left for you?"

"Because I left my cell phone home last night when we went to the movies and never bothered to check it until this morning. I saw that you called so I was just going to call you back when we got home from our hike. What are you doing here?"

"I was worried something happened to you and I know this is the route you take when you go hiking with the dog in the morning so I came out looking for you."

"What's wrong, Liddy? What's happened?"

Liddy took a deep breath. "Well, it's pretty bad."

Hayley and Gemma exchanged worried looks.

"What? Has someone died? Is it Mona?" Hayley said, suddenly concerned.

"No! It's not Mona! Although it's a miracle that woman hasn't keeled over from a coronary with all the butter and carbs she consumes!" Liddy said.

"So what? Tell us!" Gemma said, more impatient than her mother.

"Well, Sonny and I went out to dinner last night at McKay's because you know how much I love their Duck Confit Spring Rolls . . ."

"The point, Liddy. Get to the point," Hayley sighed.

"Well, who should be at the next table when we sat down but Aaron and his new lady friend."

"Please tell me that isn't why you left four frantic phone messages and came racing out here this morning nearly mowing us down!" Hayley screamed.

"Of course it is! Don't you want to know who he's dating? It was exactly who we all suspected! And now I have hard evidence! I have an eyewitness! Me!" Liddy said, perplexed as to why Hayley wasn't reacting more to this big news.

"No, Liddy. I don't. I told you I don't care."

Hayley would be lying if she didn't admit to herself that deep down on some level she was slightly curious to know, but she certainly wasn't going to allow Liddy and Gemma to see that.

"You can't be serious," Liddy said, mouth agape.

"It's none of my business . . ."

"Crystal Collier!" Liddy blurted out.

Really?

Crystal Collier?

Well, truth be told, Hayley was slightly surprised because Crystal just didn't seem to be Aaron's type. She was a local lawyer with a very tough, hard demeanor, extremely ambitious, and with a habit of being very direct with people, sometimes at the expense of their feelings.

"Sonny despises Crystal because she's stolen several of his clients, but he managed to fake it and smile and say hello as we passed by the table."

"Well, you've alerted me to this earth-shattering news so your work is done, Liddy. Thank you for sharing," Hayley said, shaking her head, trying hard to cover her amazement that Aaron was dating an obnoxious ballbuster like Crystal Collier.

"Gemma, you work so closely with Aaron I'm shocked that you didn't already know," Liddy said, eyeing her suspiciously.

"I did know," Gemma said quietly.

"Why wouldn't you tell your mother?" Liddy screamed.

"Because as I've said a hundred times it's none of my business!" Hayley yelled.

Gemma turned and put a hand on her mother's shoulder. "I didn't mention it because I didn't want to hurt your feelings."

"Gemma, there is absolutely no reason to pussy-foot around me. I can handle Aaron dating someone new. In fact, I really, truly am happy for him that he's getting out there again but . . ."

"But what?" Liddy demanded to know.

"Crystal Collier?"

"See! You're as dumbfounded as I am! How could Aaron choose a woman so aggressive and in your face? She's so not his type!"

Liddy was right.

Crystal was far from Aaron's type.

But then again how did she really know that?

Maybe Crystal was exactly the kind of woman Aaron was attracted to and it was Hayley who hadn't been his type.

That would certainly explain why their relationship didn't last.

Chapter 12

"They look adorable!" Hayley cooed as she snapped photos of Leroy and Blueberry with her iPhone later that morning.

Gemma proudly inspected her work. Leroy was dressed as a devil with red horns and a red cape and Blueberry was a witch complete with a black pointy hat and cape.

They both looked absolutely miserable and utterly humiliated.

"I have to post these photos on Facebook immediately!" Hayley said, tapping her phone excitedly.

"Cheer up, guys," Gemma said, rubbing the heads of Leroy and Blueberry, both of whom glared straight ahead silently planning on just how they were going to exact their revenge for this gross indignity. "You look so cute one of you just might win the contest."

Suddenly Danny breezed through the front door. "Hey, Gemma, awesome job! They look fantastic!"

"Thanks, Dad. I think the costume choice for

both of them was very appropriate," Gemma said, chuckling.

Hayley stared at Danny, marveling at his audacity.

He still had no concept of how to act like a proper ex-husband.

You don't just show up and enter the house without even ringing the bell.

Danny caught her looking at him exasperated.

"What?"

"You do realize you no longer live here, right?"

"Yeah. Why?"

"So usually when someone doesn't live here, they don't just barge in unannounced."

"You serious?"

Hayley stared at him until he got the message.

Danny sighed. "Fine. Next time I'll knock."

"You going to stay for dinner, Dad?" Gemma asked as she knelt down to adjust the pointy black hat on top of Blueberry's head.

"Sorry, Gem, it turns out I have to leave town a little earlier than expected," Danny said, frowning.

"What? Why?" Gemma moaned.

"Something's come up. But I couldn't leave without swinging by to say good-bye to my kids. Where's your brother?"

"Upstairs," Gemma said, standing back up and hugging her father. "I don't want you to go."

"I know. I wish I could stay too," Danny said before calling upstairs. "Hey, Tarantino, get down here and give your old man a hug good-bye!"

"This is rather sudden," Hayley said, more than a little suspicious. "Would this have anything to do with what happened at the Criterion Theatre last night?"

"Nothing happened at the theater. Everything is fine," Danny sighed.

She could tell he was lying.

She could always tell when he was lying.

He couldn't completely hide his fidgeting and twitching, which was a surefire indicator that he was a complete ball of nerves.

Dustin pounded down the stairs. "You're leaving?"

"Yeah, got to hit the road. But I'll be back, okay, bro?" Danny said, cupping a hand around Dustin's neck and drawing him in for a big bear hug. "Make sure you two look after your mom. She's getting old and won't be able to take care of herself much longer."

"That's really the last thing you're going to say before you leave?" Hayley asked, playfully slapping him on the arm.

"I'm kidding you. You've never looked younger or more beautiful," Danny said, attempting honest-to-goodness sincerity.

Hayley was just barely buying it.

But she appreciated the sentiment.

"When are you coming back?" Dustin asked.

"I don't know. Hopefully soon. But you will be the first to know," Danny said, kissing him on top of the head.

Hayley watched her kids.

They were making a real effort not to look sad and disappointed.

But it was tough because she could tell that's what they were feeling at the moment.

Their father was taking off again with promises to

return, but they had heard those words before and so they had learned to be a bit more skeptical.

They loved having their father around, and it bothered Hayley that no matter how hard she worked to protect them from getting hurt sometimes it was just impossible.

"Hey, babe, do me a favor. Say good-bye to Uncle Otis for me, will you?" Danny asked as he headed for the door.

"You didn't see him today?" Hayley asked.

"No. He never came home from his moonshine run last night," Danny said, shrugging.

"That's a little odd," Hayley said.

"Not really. Sometimes after a big sale, Otis goes on a bender to celebrate and can be gone days at a time. Trust me. I know the guy. This is not unusual behavior."

"Well, I'll be sure to tell him the next time I see him," Hayley said.

Danny stopped at the door, turned around, and then marched back and put his hands on Hayley's face. "Can I at least get a good-bye kiss?"

"On the cheek," Hayley warned.

Danny nodded, removed his hands, and kissed his ex-wife gently on the cheek, and then without another word, pivoted around and walked out of the house.

Hayley went to close the door when the police scanner on top of the refrigerator in the kitchen crackled to life and she heard the voice of the dispatcher. "All units, we have a 10-54 at the Ledgelawn Cemetery."

"That's a possible dead body," Hayley said.

Hayley's cell phone rang.

It was Randy.

She quickly answered the call.

"Hey, it's me," Randy said. "You listening to the scanner?"

"Yes. We just heard. What's going on?"

"Apparently a few kids were playing at the cemetery and stumbled across a dead body lying face down next to a tombstone. They thought it might be a Halloween prank and the guy was going to jump up and scare them, but they kicked it a few times and it looked like a real dead body so they called 911."

"That's awful. Do you they know who it is?"

"Yes. Otis Pearson."

Hayley dropped the phone and ran to the door, swinging it open in time to see Danny climbing into his rental.

"Danny, wait!"

Island Food & Spirits
by
Hayley Powell

There is nothing I enjoy more on a
chilly fall evening in October than a
good hearty bowl of Pumpkin Soup.
Even better than that, there is nothing
I enjoy more to drink while preparing
my soup than a strong Pumpkin Cocktail.

So as I downed my cocktail and
gathered my ingredients, I was reminded of a woeful tale that happened
years ago when I made my very first
batch of Pumpkin Soup. Eager to have
some taste tasters try my first attempt,
I told my husband at the time, Danny,
to invite over his uncle Otis and his
wife, Tori, since our kids were at the
time visiting their grandmother in
Florida. Otis, who didn't get invited
to many places because of his aversion
to soap and bathwater, was thrilled
and even offered to bring us a few
pumpkins that he recently "acquired."

When Danny announced Otis had offered us free pumpkins he "acquired" I was immediately suspicious. Otis, who had a long record of run-ins with the law during his youth and some years beyond, was not to be trusted. And in my mind, "acquired" was just a fancy word for *stolen*!

Danny insisted Otis had turned over a new leaf and was now a law-abiding citizen, and his past transgressions were just that . . . in the past. So I relented and they showed up at the house in their beat-up Ford truck twenty minutes later.

Danny ran outside to help Otis with the pumpkins while Tori joined me in the kitchen for one of my signature Pumpkin Cocktails.

A whole hour passed as Tori polished off three of my cocktails all the while complaining about her deadbeat husband who made her life miserable. She hardly took a breath except to slurp down her drink.

The soup was bubbling on the stove ready to be served and after another round of cocktails we were fresh out of bourbon.

I could not believe how long it was taking the boys to carry in a few pumpkins. At that moment, the police scanner sitting up on top of the refrigerator sounded off (pretty much everyone in town has one) and through the crackling we heard the dispatcher mention "Frenchman's Bay," "Coast Guard," "old Ford truck," "Fire and Rescue," "crane," and the key word, "pumpkins"!

Tori and I jumped up and shot out of the house.

Sure enough, outside there was no sign of Otis or Danny or Otis's truck and all those pumpkins. Tori and I scrambled into my car and we tore through town like a bullet train to the town pier. Tori spent the whole ride wailing about what she would do if she lost the love of her life, completely forgetting she had just spent the previous hour bashing him.

I squealed the car to a stop and slammed the gear into park once we hit the town pier, and we both jumped out and joined a large crowd gathered at the bottom of Main Street staring down into the water. I frantically pushed my way through, a sobbing Tori clinging to me all the way until we reached the edge.

We both gasped in shock at the sight of Otis's truck submerged in the water, just the back end sticking out surrounded by fifteen pumpkins floating around it. We spotted a small rescue skiff with rescue divers on board off a Coast Guard boat out in the bay heading full tilt toward the upended truck. Meanwhile, on land a large semi with a massive crane was being backed up to the end of the pier. Some firemen were setting up a few floodlights facing the water and the police force was placing barriers to keep back the crowd of onlookers.

Tori lost it, screaming over losing such a sweet and devoted husband!

I was in a state of shock.

What would I tell the kids?

They were so young.

The crowd watched me hugging Tori, all with looks of profound pity.

A few neighbors and friends who were there gave us a quick hug or offered an encouraging word.

"What's going on here?" a man behind me asked.

It was a familiar voice.

It was my Danny.

I spun around and there he was standing with Uncle Otis, craning his neck to get a good look at what everyone was staring at. He was surprised to see me. "Hey, babe, what are you doing here?"

Before I could answer him, Tori let out a shriek to rival the nine o'clock whistle and then fainted dead away to the ground. Otis remarked he had never seen her so quiet as he poked her sides with his fishing boot to revive her.

Well, it turned out, Danny and Otis conspired to take a quick trip to Geddy's Pub for a beer or two before unloading all the pumpkins. Otis parked his old junky truck on the hill across the street from the bar, pointing down toward the water, and apparently in his haste to get his hands on a cold Budweiser, put the gear in neutral instead of park. The rest, as they say, is history.

A few of my friends pointed to that night as the beginning of the end of my marriage to Danny. But it wasn't quite over yet and there would be many more stories like this to tell. But that little gem was the talk of the town all the way into the New Year until Matt Gray had a few too many beers and took his snowmobile for a midnight spin after a fresh snowfall up and down the main streets in town, leading the police on a merry chase before crashing into a snowplow. He was fine, but I must say, I was rather relieved that people finally had a new topic to discuss.

The only thing good that came out of that night was once the Coast Guard fished all those pumpkins out of the bay I had plenty extra to make more of my Pumpkin Soup and a whole season's worth of Pumpkin Cocktails!

Pumpkin Soup

<u>Ingredients</u>
6 cups chicken stock (homemade or
    store-bought)
1 ½ teaspoon salt
4 cups pumpkin puree
1 cup chopped onion
½ teaspoon thyme
1 glove garlic, minced

½ cup heavy whipping cream

In a large pot add your stock, salt,
pumpkin, onion, thyme, garlic, and pep-
percorns. Stir this all together and
bring to a boil. Reduce heat to low and
simmer for 30 minutes uncovered.

Using a blender or food processor
puree your soup a cup at a time (to
avoid splashing).

Return the soup back to the pot and
bring it to a boil again. Reduce the
heat and simmer another 30 minutes
uncovered.

Stir in your heavy whipping cream.

Pour the soup into bowls, grab a
spoon, and enjoy!

Pumpkin Cocktail

<u>Ingredients</u>
1 ½ ounces bourbon (your favorite)
½ ounce sherry
½ ounce fresh lemon juice

½ ounce simple syrup
1 teaspoon pumpkin butter (I like to
    use *Stonewall Kitchen's*)
2 dashes Angostura bitters
Cinnamon stick to garnish

Add all your ingredients to an ice-filled cocktail shaker and shake really well. Strain into an ice-filled rocks glass and garnish with a cinnamon stick.

Sit back and let this delicious fall cocktail warm you up!

Chapter 13

"Poor Uncle Otis. The old guy probably wandered into the graveyard drunk as a skunk, tripped, and banged his head on the tombstone and died," Danny said, shaking his head while standing with Hayley behind yellow police tape that had been tied around two adjacent gravestones.

Danny fancied himself an armchair detective after spending years in front of the TV drinking beer and watching *CSI* and *Law & Order* reruns.

Hayley found it annoying because he was just not very good at solving the crime despite his over-inflated ego. She remembered when they were first married they would watch a *Murder, She Wrote* episode on cable and Danny would spend the whole hour guessing every suspect questioned, and then after the delightful Angela Lansbury would unmask the killer and motive in the final segment, Danny would nod in agreement and proclaim, "See! I told you!"

Hayley would just wring her hands and keep her mouth shut in order to avoid an argument. But it took every ounce of strength not to blurt out, "You have no idea what you're talking about!"

Danny also appeared unimpressed with Hayley's recent history of investigating and solving local crimes with a striking success rate. Or if he was impressed and just not showing it, he probably figured he was the one who taught her everything she knew.

Hayley was shoved aside by a crowd of gawkers mixed with a few local reporters, who all jostled into position to get the best look at the crime scene. She elbowed one aggressive photographer sharply in the ribs who tried pushing her out of the way before realizing he freelanced for the *Island Times*.

Bar Harbor Police Chief Sergio and two of his officers, Donnie and Earl, carefully combed the blocked-off area for evidence while a forensics team examined the body and snapped pictures in order to make the determination as to just what happened to poor old Otis Pearson. Hayley scanned the scene and noticed a trail through the mud leading from the gravel path to the tombstone.

"Danny, look at that over there. There's a path through the mud but no footprints. It looks like something was dragged off the beaten path over to that row of tombstones where Otis was found. If someone dragged a body through the mud, the body would likely erase any sign of footprints."

"What are you trying to say, Hayley?" Danny asked, barely paying her any mind as he watched the forensics team in action. "Man, why didn't I become a CSI guy? I would've been so good at it."

"I'm saying maybe someone killed Otis somewhere else and drove him here in a car, and then dragged his body over there and left it to confuse the police."

"That's ridiculous, babe. Why do you automatically assume Otis was murdered? You need to stop reading so many mystery novels. Otis was a klutz and a drunk. He fell and hit his head. End of story."

Sergio wandered over to Hayley and Danny, and the obnoxious pushy photographer leaned into Hayley in order to eavesdrop on the conversation. Hayley gave him another quick jab in the ribs, and with a grunt, he moved out of her personal space.

"What's the story so far, Sergio?" Hayley asked, keeping her voice down.

"Severe trauma to the head. He definitely died from his injury. At least that's the preliminary assessment," Sergio whispered, not wanting the crowd to overhear him sharing details of an open investigation with his sister-in-law.

But of course, given Hayley's history in town, most of the crowd already assumed that was exactly what he was doing.

Danny chuckled with a self-satisfied smile. "You've got to learn to trust me, babe. Like I've been saying, he fell and hit his head on the gravestone."

"Don't gloat, Danny. It makes your smile crooked and it's really unattractive," Hayley said.

"I don't believe he fell here. I think whatever gave him the head injury happened somewhere else," Sergio said, instantly wiping the smile off Danny's face.

"What do you mean?" Danny sputtered.

"The way the body is positioned doesn't line up with him tripping and hitting his head on the flintstone."

"*The Flintstones*? What's he talking about, Hayley? Why is he talking about a cartoon? I'm confused," Danny said, turning to Hayley.

She rested a hand on his arm. "He means tombstone."

"Why didn't he say that?" Danny asked, turning back to Sergio.

"I did," Sergio seethed.

"I'm sorry to second-guess you, Sergio, but couldn't Otis have fallen over there? Maybe he was still alive and tried crawling for help and just died in that position," Danny said confidently, determined to defend his original theory.

"The mud trail that leads over to his body suggests someone dragged him from the gravel path and there are plenty of tire tracks to support the theory he was driven here," Sergio said. "No, he was brought here from somewhere else."

Officer Earl sauntered over to Sergio, rubbing his hands together and then wiping them on his pants. "You got a handkerchief or a moist wipe or something I can have to clean off my hands, Chief?"

"What the hell did you touch, Earl?" Sergio asked.

"I wanted a smoke but dropped my lighter and it fell right between the dead guy's feet and I had to move his boot to get to it—"

"You touched the body?" Sergio yelled, eyes blazing.

"Well, no . . . I . . . I mean . . . just the boot . . . I just had to get my lighter . . ."

"Have you learned nothing since you've been with the department, Earl? You never touch anything until forensics has completed their investigation.

Congratulations! You've just compromised an active crime scene!"

"Man, when you put it like that, it sounds kind of bad," Earl said softly, regretting ever admitting anything to the chief.

"So what's on your hands, Earl?" Hayley asked, noticing a green sticky goo on the tips of his fingers.

"I don't know. It was on the soles of Otis's boots. It's like glue and I can't get it off," Earl said, annoyed, keeping one eye on Sergio to gauge his anger.

"Well, go over and have forensics take a sample before you wash it off, do you think you can do that for me, Earl?" Sergio sighed.

"Yes, sir," Earl said before scampering off like a scolded child.

"I've got to get back to it. I'll see you later," Sergio said before marching back over to the dead body.

Danny watched Sergio standing over the still body of his uncle Otis a few minutes and then his eyes welled up with tears. "I can't believe he's gone, Hayley. He was my favorite uncle. We were drinking his moonshine and swapping stories just the other night and now he's gone . . . forever . . ."

Danny reached out for a comforting hug from Hayley.

She hesitated, not sure she was ready to open herself up to a tender moment with her ex-husband. Danny was a terrific actor and so there was a question of whether or not his emotions at this moment were genuine. But she decided to give him the benefit of the doubt and put her arms around him and held him close.

The *Island Times* freelance photographer took the opportunity to snap a few shots of Otis's grieving nephew. When Danny heard the flashes going off, he began wailing and putting on a good show.

Sergio noticed the commotion and made a beeline back over to them. "One thing I forgot to mention, Danny."

Danny raised his head off Hayley's shoulder but kept his arms firmly fastened around her as he sniffed. "What's that, Sergio?"

"Don't go far. I need you to stick around until we conclude our investigation."

Danny nodded, hugged Hayley tighter, and then said, "Of course, Chief. I wouldn't dream of going anywhere until we get to the truth about what happened to poor Uncle Otis."

"Good," Sergio said, before turning around and walking away again.

Danny was saying the right words, but Hayley could tell he was rattled.

He shifted nervously and kept clearing his throat.

She knew all his mannerisms from years of experience.

Danny Powell was in full-on panic mode.

And usually when that happened it wasn't long before he would disappear.

Chapter 14

Hayley pulled her car off the main road and down the dirt driveway to Otis Pearson's shack in the woods near Tremont to find a police cruiser with its blue lights flashing parked out front.

When she got out of the car and walked up the creaky wooden steps of the shack, Sergio suddenly appeared from around back to greet her.

"What are you doing here?" he asked.

"I came here to see Danny, and make sure he doesn't try to blow town before he's given the all clear. What about you?"

"I came to ask him a few questions but when I got here the door was wide open and there didn't appear to be anyone inside. I was just checking around back to see if he was chopping wood for the fireplace or something."

Hayley laughed to herself over the idea of Danny chopping wood.

He wasn't a man who was rejuvenated by manual labor.

He usually bought the wood with Hayley's money.

Or stole a few logs from the neighbor's pile.

"Come on, let's go inside," Sergio said, leading the way.

Hayley followed close on his heels.

Sergio stopped in the doorway and looked around at the mess.

There were rat droppings in the corner next to the couch and flies buzzed around the dirty dishes piled high in the sink and the fireplace was caked in soot.

Plaid shirts and stained underwear were draped over a couple of rickety chairs and some moonshine jugs were upended on their sides on the floor.

Sergio shook his head, disgusted. "Looks like the place has been torn apart and ransacked."

Hayley snorted. "Uh, no, this is just how Otis keeps house. The place looks exactly the same as when I was last here, which was only a few days ago."

Sergio stared at her in disbelief.

Sergio led her over to the sectioned-off area where Otis slept. The dirty, musty mattress on the floor had been violently ripped open.

There were chunks of yellow foam strewn everywhere.

"Was that mattress in such a sorry state when you were last here?" Sergio asked, eyebrow raised.

"No. Other than those nasty stains it was pretty much intact."

"Then someone *has* been here. Any idea what he or she might have been looking for?"

"I'm afraid so. Otis doesn't believe in banks. He told me he stashes his savings, something like forty grand, in that mattress."

Sergio's mind raced. "So if the rest of the place looks exactly the same as when you were here previously, and only the mattress appears to have been disturbed, then whoever came here and stole Otis's money knew exactly what he or she was looking for and where to find it."

Hayley walked over and inspected the mutilated mattress.

It made sense.

Sergio moved up behind her. "Who else besides you knew Otis kept his money in there?"

Hayley winced.

Just like Lucy Ricardo used to do when she didn't want to admit something to her Cuban bandleader husband.

"Hayley . . ." Sergio said, drawing her name out just like Ricky Ricardo when he would say, "Lucy . . ."

He even had the Desi Arnaz accent to boot.

Except it was Brazilian instead of Cuban, but still, it was close enough.

Sergio turned Hayley around and stared at her with the serious, commanding police chief look he often used to intimidate people. "Did Danny know about the money in the mattress?"

Hayley nodded.

She couldn't believe it.

She didn't want to believe it.

Could Danny have killed his own uncle for forty grand?

She couldn't even entertain the possibility.

But it wasn't looking too good for him at the moment.

Sergio gripped her shoulders.

"Where is he?"

Hayley shrugged. "I . . . I don't know. I thought he would be here . . ."

But a part of her knew exactly where her troublesome ex-husband was right now.

Probably hightailing it out of town.

If he wasn't already across state lines.

If he was as guilty

Chapter 15

"He's guilty, Hayley," Bruce said, stuffing an onion
bagel slathered in cream cheese into his mouth, and
then wiping a smudge of cheese off the corner of his
lip with his tongue. "And the sooner you come to
accept it, the easier it will be."

Danny wasn't the only one who considered himself a crack detective.

Bruce Linney, too, had come to believe he was as
observant and sharp and adept at deductive reasoning as any Arthur Conan Doyle creation.

Hayley let out a sigh behind her desk at the *Island
Times* office and tried to focus on items left to do in
her in-box.

"Danny adored his uncle Otis, Bruce," Hayley
said, not entirely comfortable being the lone de-
fender of her ex-husband. "Why would he want to
kill him?"

Danny stuffed the rest of his bagel in his mouth.
"To get his grubby hands on his uncle's money! You
just don't want to see the truth. I'm sorry, Hayley.

In my experienced view, this is pretty much an easy, open-and-shut case."

"Stop talking with your mouth full, Bruce. Didn't your mother ever teach you manners?"

Bruce wiped his mouth with his forearm. "Don't try changing the subject. You know I'm right."

Hayley swiveled around in her office chair and glared at him. "You always do this, Bruce. You always go with the obvious theory. That's why you're so wrong all the time."

"*Wrong*? When am I wrong . . ." Bruce swallowed the last word because he knew he was setting himself up for a humiliating rundown of all the recent local-crime cases where he had pointed his finger at the wrong person.

Hayley was tempted.

She desperately wanted to put him in his place and make him feel small for not considering how she was feeling about the mounting evidence against her ex.

But instead, once again, she found herself rushing to Danny's defense. "My ex-husband may be a liar and a cheat and a cad, but that doesn't make him a murderer."

"But you always said he was terrible with money, and would often borrow from questionable sources, and wind up getting himself in some pretty major debt. What if he got desperate? What if he needed a wad of cash and fast? He knew where he could find forty grand. That much money could fix a lot of problems."

Hayley felt her whole face flush with rage.

Bruce was being insensitive to how she was

feeling and wholly ignorant of how his casual, off-the-cuff deductions were hurting her deeply.

She suddenly lashed out. "What's your problem, Bruce?"

"Problem. I don't have a—"

"Are you jealous?"

Bruce scoffed. "Jealous? Jealous of what?"

Hayley stopped herself.

She couldn't believe what she had just said.

Bruce was still playing catch-up.

He was confused.

She decided to let it go.

And hope what she was implying wouldn't dawn on him.

"Why would I be jealous of—?"

And then, of course, it dawned on him.

"Are you saying . . . ? Oh, Hayley, really. You think I'm jealous because of *you* . . . ? That's . . . that's crazy . . ."

"I didn't say me. You said me. All I meant was Danny is handsome and charming and women seem to love him and sometimes other men resent that. I never mentioned me specifically."

Bruce raised a hand in protest. "You implied it! You did!"

There was an awkward silence.

Hayley was waiting for Bruce to deny he was jealous because of Danny's relationship with Hayley.

But he didn't.

He just stood there not knowing what to say.

The tension lingered for a few more uncomfortable moments.

Luckily the door to the office blew open and Sergio walked in with Danny.

"Hey, babe. Miss me?" he said, his megawatt smile on full display.

Bruce sighed and rolled his eyes.

Danny threw his arms around Sergio. "Hey, man, thanks for the ride."

Sergio kept his arms at his side, refusing to hug Danny back.

"So I guess the Bar Harbor Police Department is now a taxi service," Bruce said mockingly.

"I didn't just give him a free ride," Sergio said, doing a slow burn. "I had Officers Donnie and Earl stationed at the Trenton Bridge to make sure Danny didn't try leaving, and sure enough, they intercepted him trying to get off the island in his rental car."

"Danny!" Hayley hollered.

"Everybody calm down. I wasn't trying to blow town. I was just going shopping at the Bangor Mall to buy some presents for my kids."

Hayley, Bruce, and Sergio just stared at him.

He wasn't fooling anyone.

Sensing he had no supporters, Danny rushed up to Sergio and grabbed him by his thick, muscled arms. "Trust me, Sergio. I am not going anywhere until we get to the bottom of my dear uncle's senseless death. You can trust me. We're family."

"Please don't touch me, Danny," Sergio said quietly.

Danny continued to grasp Sergio's rock-hard biceps. "I love you, man. It kills me that you don't believe me."

Sergio glared at Danny's hands gripping his arms. "I'm not going to tell you again. Don't make me hit you."

Danny let go and held up his hands, fingers splayed

open, defeated. "You're like impenetrable. Most gay guys love it when I flirt with them."

"Oh, Danny . . ." Hayley said, shaking her head, embarrassed.

"I'm going to keep an eye on you, Danny," Sergio said. "So don't try anything stupid."

Danny nodded, annoyed that Sergio was immune to his charms.

"If I had the manpower, I'd keep a man posted at your uncle's shack to make doubly sure you don't try to go anywhere again."

Danny smiled. "There's no need to have an officer tail me. It's a complete waste of resources. I'm not a flight risk."

"Shut up, Danny," Hayley said.

Danny retreated like a chastised boy and stared at his shoes.

"Maybe you could help me out, Hayley," Sergio said.

"Me? How?"

"Maybe Danny could stay with you. That way you could keep an eye on him."

Danny perked up again. "That is an excellent idea, Chief!"

"No! Absolutely not! That's a terrible idea!"

Danny grabbed Hayley's hands and pulled them toward his chest, resting her fingers upon his heart. "Babe, please. I can't stay at that shack. What if the killer is lurking around Tremont and attacks me in that remote cabin in the woods where I am all alone and defenseless?"

"That's the biggest bunch of bull pucky you've ever come up with, Danny!" Hayley yelled, not at all willing to go along with this cockamamy plan.

"Hayley's right! It's the worst idea I've ever heard!" Bruce blurted out.

At least Bruce was in her corner.

But it made her wonder why.

"Please, Hayley, I have nowhere else to go . . ." Danny begged with his big puppy-dog eyes.

"Stop being so melodramatic! You're not staying with me!" Hayley said before turning to Sergio. "Why can't he stay with you and Randy?"

This caught Sergio off guard.

His mind raced to come up with a valid excuse.

But he couldn't and he was starting to panic.

Danny finally came to his rescue.

"I can't sleep in a strange house. Not after the trauma I've just been through. Losing a close relative under such violent and emotionally wrenching circumstances. I need familiarity. I need people around me that I love and trust. I need my kids."

The kids.

That was his secret weapon.

Hayley had always felt guilty after the divorce keeping the kids in Maine with her while Danny moved to Iowa.

He may have been a lousy husband but he was a loving and devoted father.

And he actually resembled a kind and thoughtful and caring human being whenever he was around Gemma and Dustin.

And he knew in his gut that would get to Hayley.

She was wavering.

And she hated herself for it.

"Please," Danny said in a quiet and reasonable tone. "It's just for a few days until they clear me. I'll be on my best behavior."

He knew she was going to cave.

But he waited patiently for her to say it out loud.

"Okay," Hayley whispered.

Danny had to refrain from whooping and hollering.

Hayley wagged a finger at him. "You sleep on the couch."

"Of course. This is going to be great. Just like old times."

He gave her a quick peck on the cheek.

"Yes. Old times," Hayley said, "when we'd have a big fight and I'd make you sleep on the couch."

Danny was euphoric.

Sergio was relieved.

Bruce was apoplectic but struggled to conceal it.

And Hayley just had a huge sense of dread.

Chapter 16

"I really shouldn't discuss this, Hayley," Tori Pearson said as she ushered Hayley inside her small studio apartment that was part of a low-income housing unit situated in a wooded area off the West Street extension on the outskirts of town. "My doctor warned me when I talked about Otis I risked raising my blood pressure and that does nothing to help my diabetes and anxiety issues."

Tori Pearson was Otis's ex-wife, a short, stout woman with prematurely graying hair that was chopped off short to make her look like a women's prison guard.

She was also, like her ex-husband, a slob.

Her packed living quarters was bursting with knickknacks and furniture from Goodwill that was too big for the space.

"How do you like the place?" Tori asked, beaming. "I just got approved to move in a few weeks ago."

"It looks lovely," Hayley lied.

Tori led her into the small kitchenette and pointed to some curtains with poodles on them in the tiny window. "Aren't those curtains adorable? I got them for five dollars at a yard sale last weekend!"

"I love them!" Hayley lied again.

Hayley loved dogs but she could never imagine herself accenting her kitchen with such a gaudy print.

There was a musty odor permeating through out the tiny, stifling apartment.

"I'm thinking of selling my car," Tori said suddenly, frowning.

"Oh. Okay."

That was the best Hayley could come up with as a response since the topic had seemed to come out of nowhere.

"My health insurance doesn't cover the cost of my medications anymore and I've already maxed out my credit cards so I need to do something. Otherwise I won't be able to afford my meds and then I will get sick and die and then where will I be?"

"Well, at least selling your car will give you some cash flow."

"Not that the damn clunker is worth much, but it'll get me by for at least a few more months. It hasn't been easy for me, Hayley," Tori whined. "With all my health issues and my money problems and the government assistance I receive which doesn't go very far and then there's my mother who refuses to help me anymore . . . my own mother . . . I guess you can't count on anyone . . ."

Hayley wanted to suggest to Tori that perhaps she should consider going out and getting a job but she held her tongue.

"And now my back is acting up," Tori groaned, her body hunched over. "I have this sharp, constant pain. It's excruciating. I can hardly move anymore."

"Well, I'm sorry to hear about all you're going through and the last thing I want to do is take up too much of your time so I'll get right to the point. I'm here about Otis . . ."

Tori suddenly snapped to attention.

She stood erect, back pain be damned.

There was a frightening flash of anger on her face as all her ailments seemed to miraculously melt away at the mention of her ex-husband.

"Why would I possibly want to talk about that good-for-nothing low-life piece of trash?"

"Well, I'm sure you heard he recently died. I mean, it's all over town."

"Of course I heard. I even did a little jig right here in the middle of my living room to celebrate."

"And that someone murdered him . . . ?"

"Yes! Yes, I read all about it in Bruce Linney's column. And let me tell you, I will not rest until I find the person responsible for splattering Otis's brains all over the Ledgelawn Cemetery . . ."

Finally.

A little compassion.

"Because I want to shake that hero's hand. He's done the world an immeasurable service."

Never mind.

"You have no idea what that man put me through, Hayley," Tori said, stirring herself up into a frenzy. "He ruined my life. When he walked out on me, he left me high and dry. With no way to pay my bills. No way to take care of myself."

Again.

There was always the job listings section in the *Island Times*.

Very easy to read.

Hayley organized the page herself.

But that solution seemed a little too daunting for Tori Pearson.

"I was so stricken by him deserting me, I started having unexpected anxiety attacks. All the time. Day and night. I had trouble leaving the house. I was an acrobatic."

"You mean agoraphobic?"

Sergio may have found his match for all those malapropisms.

"Whatever. You know, I tried working part-time last summer, you know, to at least make a little extra money to pay for my wine I drink every night during Greta Van Susteren. I got a few shifts in a gift shop as a cashier but when I tried to open the register I kept forgetting which button to push. I got so nervous and upset I just walked right out of the shop and never went back."

"I'm sorry you had to go through that, Tori," Hayley said, wondering at this point why she was even here indulging this lazy, self-absorbed woman.

"I called Otis," she said breathlessly. "I was hoping he might take pity on me and send me a few dollars but that bastard didn't even care. He just said he was broke and couldn't help me. That bastard left me to fend for myself! I never recovered. And here I am in this ghastly state of despair."

In a nice studio apartment.

With cable TV.

And poodle curtains.

She really didn't have too much to complain about.

"You say Otis was broke?"

"Yes. That layabout didn't even try to get a job in order to help me! Don't you hate people who don't take responsibility for their lives and responsibilities?"

The irony of her statement was completely lost on her.

"Well, it turns out Otis did save some money right before he died," Hayley said.

"I'm sure that was from his illegal moonshine business. He always told me he was going to strike it big with that god-awful booze he cooked up in the backyard." Tori checked her watch. "Excuse me. It's time to take my pills."

She crossed to the kitchen and opened a small plastic container and plucked out four pills.

A white one.

A blue one.

A red one.

And a green one.

Then she filled a glass with some cranberry juice from the refrigerator.

"He kept the cash hidden in a mattress," Hayley said.

"How much did he have?"

"Forty grand."

"How much?"

Tori popped the pills into her mouth and chased them down with the juice.

"Forty grand."

Tori spit out the cranberry juice, spraying it all over her poodle-print curtains.

"How . . . ? Forty grand? Are you serious?"

"So I take it you knew nothing about it."

"Of course I didn't! Forty grand? That lying cheat! I'm not surprised he was squirreling money away and not telling me about it. He was always afraid I'd go after him for alimony, but I gave up expecting any kind of support from him years ago even when we were still married."

"Tori, do you know of anyone, anyone you can remember, who had it out for Otis and might have wanted to do him some harm?"

"You mean besides *me*?"

"Yes."

"Well, let me think . . ."

She thought long and hard, her eyes flitting from side to side, her lips pursed.

And then she turned back to Hayley.

"To be honest, I can't think of anyone. He was a frustrating, irresponsible drunk, but at the end of the day he was still a lovable drunk. As much as I hate to admit it, people enjoyed having him around. He was a great storyteller and boy, could he tell a good dirty joke."

Hayley smiled, remembering some of those family gatherings when she was still married to Danny when Otis would get sloshed and stand up and start rattling off a slew of jokes that were so blue she had to scoot her two kids out of the room.

"Actually the only person who comes to mind is that good-for-nothing nephew of his. I heard he's back in town skulking about, figuring out his next scheme . . . You know the one I'm talking about . . . real scummy kind of guy . . ."

Hayley shifted uncomfortably.

Tori glanced at her and then her face fell.

"Oh dear Lord, how could I be so dumb?"

"Really. It's okay. We're not married anymore."

"It's just been so long and he's had so many women since you two got divorced and I just sort of plum forgot you two had ever been married. How could I forget such a thing?"

Probably because it would require her to stop thinking about herself.

Hayley didn't say that.

But she really, really wanted to say that.

"Well, I don't mean to throw Danny under the bus," Tori said, backpedaling. "He's not that bad. I mean, he does have a few decent qualities . . . I'm sure we can come up with at least one if we put our heads together . . ."

"Seriously. You don't have to . . ."

"I got one! He's awfully good-looking, that's a start . . ."

Hayley nodded. "Yes. Yes, he is . . ."

"Come on, I'm sure we can come up with one more . . ."

"Tori, I'm acutely aware of the kind of man my ex-husband is. I lived with him for ten years. But I am also relatively confident he's innocent of Otis's murder."

"Of course you're right, Hayley. You asked me to think of someone and his name just kind of popped into my head. I'm so, so sorry."

"I should go. It was nice seeing you again, Tori."

What's one more little lie?

Hayley was telling the truth about Danny.

She was confident he was innocent.

But on the other hand, it had been years since she had last seen him.

And there was no telling what changes he might have gone through during that period.

Did she really truly know him anymore?

Chapter 17

The Halloween pet costume contest at Dr. Aaron Palmer's veterinary office was an all-out nail-biter after the final votes were cast.

The tally of the results revealed a tie between two entries. Splitting the vote right down the middle was Leroy in his devil costume looking adorable and Edna's Boston terrier, Emmett, in a cute Santa's elf getup.

Gemma and Edna stood side by side, the tension between them palpable as they held their respective pets in their arms, giving the small crowd gathered in the reception area one last look.

Nobody planned for what would happen if there was a tie so the final arbiter was Dr. Aaron himself, who stopped and inspected both costumes thoroughly.

Gemma was bouncing up and down with anticipation.

Leroy was a shoo-in.

The detail of his costume was far superior to the

crepe paper and Scotch tape Edna had used to throw together Emmett's bush league outfit.

Aaron turned to the crowd. "I've made my decision. The winner of a three-month supply of doggy treats and a fifty-dollar gift certificate to Petco is . . ."

Gemma took a step forward, kissing Leroy's whiskers.

"Emmett the elf dog!"

The crowd applauded warmly.

Gemma froze, in a state of shock, mouth agape, a disbelieving look on her face.

Edna fought back tears as she squeezed her tiny Boston terrier to her bosom, overwhelmed by the moment before hugging Dr. Aaron.

Not wanting to appear a spoilsport, Hayley clapped loudly for Edna's not so well-deserved victory.

Mona wasn't so politically correct. She swooped in next to Hayley and said in a far too loud voice, "Gemma was robbed!"

Hayley nudged Mona in the side with her elbow and tried to shush her.

"It was rigged, I'm telling you. I can feel it in my bones. I mean come on, Blueberry didn't even make the final five."

Hayley glanced down at the pet carrier she was holding. Inside, Blueberry hissed as if on cue to voice his own displeasure. He had been knocked out early, garnering very few votes no doubt due in part to his nasty, unappealing personality, which his colorful clown costume, a last-minute change from his original witch's outfit when Leroy chewed up the pointy hat, did very little to hide.

Gemma marched over to her mother and muttered

under her breath, "I can't believe he picked Emmett over Leroy! See? He has it out for me. He hates me!"

"I thought I taught you to be a gracious loser," Hayley said, glancing around to make sure Dr. Aaron wasn't within earshot.

"Yes, but you also taught me to stand up to injustice, and this is an outright injustice!" Gemma said, gently scratching Leroy's face as he snuggled in her arms.

"Hear, hear," Mona concurred.

"Mona, don't encourage her!" Hayley warned.

The door to the reception area flew open and Danny rushed in, stopping only to stomp the mud off his boots on the welcome mat with cat faces on it. He then raced over to Hayley and Gemma.

"Did I miss it? Did you win?"

Gemma shook her head, disappointed.

"What? I don't believe it! Who had a better costume than Leroy?"

Gemma pointed to Emmett who was lapping water out of a bowl and getting his headpiece all wet.

"You can't be serious!" Danny cried.

"Would you all please keep your voices down?" Hayley begged. "Otherwise we're going to win the award for worst family!"

From across the room, Aaron caught Hayley's eye. They smiled at each other.

But the moment was quickly shattered by Danny, who stepped in front of Hayley and blocked her view. "Anybody hungry? How about some nachos at Geddy's? My treat."

"Yes! I'm starving!" Mona said, rubbing her belly.

Danny raised an eyebrow.

He clearly hadn't meant to include her.

"By the way, why were you late?" Hayley asked.

"Oh . . . I ran into some buddies I hadn't seen in a while and we had a couple of beers and I guess I just sort of lost track of time . . ."

"What buddies?"

"You don't know them."

"You may be surprised. I pretty much know everybody in town. Why don't you try me?"

Danny shrugged. "They're from Bangor. Don't tell me you know *everybody* in Bangor."

He locked eyes with Hayley defiantly.

"Don't worry. I met them right here in town. I never tried leaving the island," Danny sighed.

He wasn't going to give up any more information.

She knew he was lying.

But now was not the time to confront him.

Instead she reached out and stroked Leroy's tummy as he relaxed in the crook of Gemma's arms. "First runner-up. Not half bad, Leroy."

Leroy tried to get the devil's horns off his head with his paws.

He was done being a show dog.

"I can tell you're miserable with those horns, Leroy. Let me help you," Hayley said, turning to Danny. "Can you hold the carrier for me, please?"

"No. That cat hates me."

"That cat hates everybody. You're not that special. Hold the damn thing, will you, please?" Hayley said, sighing.

Everything was a battle.

Just like when they were married.

Danny shrugged and took the carrier from Hayley, but it bounced a bit in the transition and Blueberry hissed again, baring his teeth through the steel mesh.

Aaron suddenly appeared next to Hayley and touched her arm. "Sorry to interrupt."

"No. Not at all," Hayley said, smiling, taking in his familiar cologne that used to drive her wild when he would show up at her house.

"We were just discussing the surprising outcome of the contest," Danny said, standing up straight, head back, like a rooster.

Aaron nodded and smiled. "I know. I've gotten a few comments."

"So what kind of pictures does Edna have of you, Doc? I'm guessing they're real nasty," Danny said, sneering.

"Danny!" Hayley shouted, ready to open the pet carrier and unleash Blueberry on him.

Maybe an armful of scratches might teach him a lesson in good manners.

"I totally get what you're saying. And I agree with you one hundred percent. I purposely chose Emmett over Leroy as the winner," Aaron said softly.

"What?" Gemma gasped.

"I know it's unfair, but life's been a little rough for Edna lately. She pretty much has been running this place, and then you came along, Gemma. You're so efficient and so talented and so young and suddenly I began relying on you for everything, completely ignoring Edna, who has been with me since I opened my practice. We all know she hardly has any friends, no family, just her dog, Emmett, and this job. She has very little going on in her life. Whereas you have everything in front of you. You're going to be a very successful veterinarian."

"Of course she is. She gets all her talent from me," Danny said, chest puffed out.

"Shut up, Danny," Hayley said, shaking her head.

Dr. Aaron put a hand on Gemma's shoulder. "I just hope you don't set up shop here in Bar Harbor because you'll probably run my business right into the ground."

"You bet she will!" Danny barked before Hayley pressed the heel of her boot down hard on his toes until he finally got the hint and clammed up.

"I had no idea . . ." Gemma said, touched by his sincerity.

Hayley was touched too.

She had forgotten about Aaron's inherent sweetness and kindness.

Danny couldn't take it anymore. He just had to pipe up again. "I don't see why anybody should get special treatment. Sometimes life just isn't fair."

"You're right, Danny. I was probably wrong to let Edna's dog win. But in the scheme of things, I figured it was just a silly little contest and I knew it would mean so much to her," Aaron said.

"I'm glad you chose Emmett. Really, I am," Gemma said, smiling, flush with excitement over her boss's glowing compliments.

"I knew you could handle it," Aaron said, patting her on the back.

"Better than her parents, that's for sure," Hayley said, eyeing Danny before turning and smiling at Dr. Aaron.

Their eyes held a gaze for a moment.

Maybe a moment too long.

Hayley looked deep into his eyes.

Was there a hint of regret in them?

Had they completely moved on from each other?
Were they truly over each other?

Danny, disturbed by what he was watching, tried to break it up with a loud hacking cough. "Excuse me."

But it didn't work.

Even Gemma noticed and looked away, pretending she wasn't aware of what was happening.

But then, out of nowhere, Crystal Collier, the aggressive, ballsy lawyer who was, according to Liddy's firsthand eyewitness account, dating Dr. Aaron, appeared and slipped her arm through Aaron's and possessively drew him close to her side.

"What did I miss?" Crystal purred, glaring at Hayley with a look that pretty much said *keep your hooks out of my man*.

"Crystal, do you know Hayley Powell?" Aaron asked. "And her husband, Danny?"

"*Ex*-husband," Hayley said, a bit too quickly.

Danny grimaced at the swiftness of her clarification.

"I know her by reputation," Crystal said coldly.

"Yikes. Now I'm worried," Hayley laughed, trying to keep the conversation light and ignore Crystal's obvious disdain for her.

"I've read a few of her columns. I'd try one or two of your recipes if I wasn't so busy. But to be honest, they're all so fattening and I try to focus on healthier options," Crystal said, her words dripping with judgment.

"What can I say? I love to eat," Hayley said, rubbing her belly.

"I can see that," Crystal said in the most disparaging tone she would muster.

There was an awkward silence.

Hayley just wanted the floor to open up and swallow her whole at this point.

Crystal finally broke the tension as she squeezed Aaron's arm. "Darling, we're going to be late for our dinner reservation."

"Right. We better go. You all have a good night. Gemma, I'll see you tomorrow," Aaron said.

As she whisked Aaron away, Crystal never relaxed her grip on his arm.

She was clearly warning off anyone who might try to foolishly trespass onto her territory.

Gemma watched them go and then muttered, "What a bitch."

"Gemma, you know I don't like you calling anyone that," Hayley said.

"Your mother's right, Gemma," Danny scolded. "It's not a nice word and I don't want to hear my daughter using it. So I will. That woman's a grade-A all-out first-prize-winning bitch!"

Gemma laughed.

Even Hayley couldn't help but chuckle.

"And if there was ever any doubt, that woman has *nothing* on you, babe," Danny said, snaking an arm around her lower back. "You are one hot mama and she's just jealous!"

"Thank you, Danny," Hayley said, letting her guard down just a bit.

"You're welcome. Now let's go get some nachos. Oh, FYI, your couch is murdering my back. Is there anywhere else you might consider letting me sleep tonight?" Danny asked, trying to be offhanded and casual.

Hayley's guard went right back up.

"You mean like my bed?"

"Well, if that's an invitation . . ."

"I'm inviting you to sleep on the floor," Hayley said, shaking her head.

"Can't blame a guy for trying."

Island Food & Spirits
by
Hayley Powell

A few Sundays ago, I was having trouble gearing up for some serious fall housecleaning so I decided to have a shot of caffeine to rev up the old engine. I wasn't in the mood for plain old boring black coffee so instead I went all out and make a festive Pumpkin Spiced Coffee with a touch of Kahlúa to put an extra little pep in my morning step.

Well, that drink certainly bolstered my energy all right. But not to clean the house. Pretty soon I found myself making a batch of Pumpkin Pancakes. My kids weren't even home so I ended up eating them all myself.

By lunchtime, I was lying prone on the couch, moaning from overstuffing myself and then nodding off to sleep for an unscheduled midday nap.

When I woke up, it was well past

three in the afternoon. My belly was still full and I was feeling lazy, but I knew the house wouldn't clean itself. I was in desperate need of some fresh air and exercise to clear the mind and get my muscles working for the daunting job ahead.

So I called my buddy Mona and convinced her to come with me on a three-and-a-half-mile walk around Witch Hole Pond in Acadia National Park. Since it was flat and there were no hills, Mona begrudgingly agreed to accompany me.

It was a crisp November afternoon. We were walking at a leisurely pace, admiring the breathtaking views and catching up on some local gossip. There weren't a lot of people out circling the pond.

A couple walking their dog.

A family bundled up in winter coats and gloves on one last bicycle ride before storing them until spring.

And one lone hiker with a fur hat pulled low over his ears and covering most of his face to ward off the cold. He kept his head down when he passed by us in the opposite direction.

We were about three quarters of the way around the pond when we realized we needed to pick up our pace as the sun was already beginning to set and Mona didn't want to get caught on the trail after dark, especially since she had a crippling fear of bears. Once when she was six, a man dressed up as Smokey the Bear for the firemen's parade tried giving her a piece of candy and she got so scared she threw up all over him.

Even though she had nothing to worry about because bears rarely came out of the woods onto a park trail, Mona was starting to panic. And the more jittery she got and talked about encountering one, the more nervous I actually started to get.

We were almost back around to the car when Mona stopped suddenly.

"Did you hear that?"

"Hear what?"

We heard some rustling.

Like an animal approaching.

"That!" Mona screamed.

We started walking faster and faster.

Darkness was rapidly falling upon us.

We heard more rustling and stopped in our tracks.

We looked around and then, out of nowhere, we heard something fast approaching us in the dark.

We both screamed and took off running, our arms flailing.

Whatever was behind us was gaining on us.

When we reached my car, I didn't even have time to fish out my keys, but luckily I had forgotten to lock the doors so we jumped in, heaving and panting since neither of us was in tip-top shape. I scrambled to manually lock all the doors to keep the creature out.

"It was a bear, I swear it was a bear!" Mona yelled, almost crying.

"Let's just get out of here!"

And then, something was at the driver's side door pounding on the window.

Mona and I screamed bloody murder.

"It's trying to get in the car to maul us to death!" Mona wailed.

We had both seen Leonardo DiCaprio torn up to pieces in that movie *The Revenant* and were sure we were about to suffer the same fate.

Mona had her whole head in her lap, covering it with her hands, praying the Maine black bear would not figure out how to open the door.

And then I heard the bear say something like, "Please, I just need to talk to you."

Wait, the bear said that?

I turned and looked out the driver's side window.

It was the man in the fur hat we had passed on the trail.

And he was holding my car keys up in his gloved hand.

I must have dropped them on the trail during our walk.

He quietly explained that he found them on the path and backtracked to see if they were mine, since he had only seen two cars in the parking lot next to the bridge that crossed to the park trail and one was his. When he caught up to us, we just ran away from him.

I gratefully accepted my keys back and apologized profusely to the man for running away. If not for him, we would have been stuck out all night in the dark with all those marauding Maine black bears.

Now Mona and I always make sure we do our walking when there are plenty of hours of sunlight left!

Here is a great weekend cocktail to kick off your day and a hearty, mouth-watering breakfast dish to fuel you up before you head out the door for your own refreshing walk.

Just make sure you allow yourself plenty of daylight time.

Pumpkin Spiced Coffee with Kahlúa

Ingredients

4 ounces hot coffee

1 ounce Kahlúa pumpkin spiced
    liqueur

½ ounce vodka

1 ounce milk

In your favorite coffee mug pour all of the ingredients and stir them together. For an extra treat you can always add a dollop of whipped cream and a cinnamon stick on a cold, crisp day.

Pumpkin Pancakes

<u>Ingredients</u>
⅓ cup all-purpose flour
⅓ cup whole wheat flour
½ teaspoon baking powder
½ teaspoon baking soda
2 tablespoons sugar
¼ teaspoon ground cinnamon
¼ teaspoon pumpkin pie spice
Pinch of salt
1 large egg
½ cup of milk
⅓ cup vanilla yogurt
⅓ cup pumpkin puree
1 tablespoon vegetable oil
½ teaspoon vanilla
Maple syrup

In a bowl whisk together the first eight ingredients. In another bowl mix the egg, milk, yogurt, pumpkin puree, oil, and vanilla. Add this to your dry mixture and stir in until just moistened.

Spray your griddle with cooking spray and heat to medium heat. Pour the batter by ½ cupful onto your hot griddle and cook until the tops are bubbly and the bottoms are browned. Flip and cook until golden brown. Top with maple syrup and enjoy!

Chapter 18

"Norman Cross . . . the author?" Hayley asked, looking up from her desktop computer at Bruce Linney, who hovered over her desk, smirking, rather pleased with himself.

"Yes. I did some digging and it turns out Otis Pearson's number-one moonshine client is the reclusive Master of Horror himself," Bruce said.

Norman Cross was a fan of Otis's moonshine?

"And Otis made a delivery to Cross's mansion the same night he was found in the cemetery?" Hayley asked.

"Yes. So Cross may have been the last person to see Otis alive."

"Good job, Bruce."

"I finally seem to be earning my stripes back as a relevant investigative journalist. It's been a while."

"It's like riding a bike. You never really forget how to do it," Hayley said, going back to her computer to put the final touches on tomorrow's column.

She heard Bruce quietly chuckling to himself.

"What's so amusing?"

He snapped to attention, surprised she caught him in a moment of reverie.

"What do you mean?" he asked.

"You're laughing. I'm just curious what you're thinking about."

"Nothing," Bruce said, trying to brush it off.

Hayley decided to press him. "Come on. Tell me."

Bruce seemed to be debating with himself on how to respond, but then he just shrugged and said, "It's just nice seeing you impressed."

"Impressed?"

"For years whenever you looked at me, I could see your irritation or exasperation or even boredom, and I kind of eventually got used to it, but today, for the first time, you actually seem impressed."

"That's because your skills as a reporter impressed me."

"Right. And that's why I'm happy. It feels good."

Hayley was certainly not used to Bruce being so open and honest with her.

Usually he would go to great lengths to make himself look self-assured and confident and unfazed by her sometimes critical opinion of ninety percent of his words and deeds.

But lately they had established a more friendly rapport.

And she liked it.

"I'm going to go question Mr. Cross about Otis Pearson at his house," Bruce said. "Care to join me?"

Norman Cross resided in a hilltop mansion, very old and weathered and spooky.

The perfect home base for the Master of Horror.

The kind of house you would probably find the *Scooby Doo* gang poking around in for clues.

Bats flying around.

Creepy noises.

Faint haunting screams in the distance.

Okay, so most of that was imagined but it still was old and gothic and ominous after dark.

"So what do you say?" Bruce asked.

"Why not?" Hayley said, shutting down her computer and grabbing her bag from underneath the desk.

"See? I told you we make a great team!"

"Let's not get ahead of ourselves, okay, Bruce?"

"Got it."

Chapter 19

When Hayley walked up the creaky steps onto the porch of Norman Cross's mansion with its rotted wood and peeling paint, she felt a shiver down her spine.

Bruce was hovering next to her, looking around, a little weirded out by their eerie surroundings.

This was exactly the effect Norman Cross was going for when visitors came calling.

When Hayley pressed the doorbell, she hardly expected creepy organ music right out of *The Addams Family*, but then again she had seen Cross many times in TV interviews, and he seemed to relish his role of eccentric author with a love of the macabre, the scare maestro of Mount Desert Island.

With thirty-four best sellers, he could afford a face-lift on his dilapidated three-story house, but a fresh coat of paint and a new roof along with some sensible landscaping just might hurt the brand he had worked so hard to build. Better to leave his home in a state of disarray in order to frighten passersby, his spooky reputation fully intact.

A young man opened the door and greeted them with a crooked smile. He was blond, muscular, in his mid-twenties, good-looking in an offbeat sort of way, his longish hair almost covering his piercing green eyes. "Hello, I'm Shane Hardy, Mr. Cross's writing assistant."

Bruce introduced himself and Hayley, and then Shane ushered them inside.

"Can I offer you something to drink? Coffee, hot chocolate, lemonade? Perhaps something stronger?" Shane said, winking conspiratorially.

"No, thank you," Hayley answered for both of them.

Bruce frowned.

He was a big fan of day drinking.

"We just need a few minutes of Mr. Cross's time," Bruce said.

"Yes, of course. Let me go up and tell him you're here. He's working in his office," Shane said, pulling some strands of his long blond hair out of his face and then bounding up the grand staircase.

Bruce and Hayley look around.

There were a lot of framed book covers of Norman Cross's past work hanging on the walls.

"I remember reading that one in high school," Hayley said, pointing to one cover.

"*Blades*? What was it about?"

"A possessed lawn mower."

"Are you serious? I was thinking it might be about a demented ice skater."

"Nope. Lawn mower. It scared the daylights out of me. I couldn't sleep for a week. Let alone go out in our backyard or even touch any of my father's gardening tools."

"I was a little more high-minded in my literary pursuits," Bruce scoffed.

"I've seen what you read, Bruce. James Patterson isn't exactly Tolstoy!"

Hayley continued down the line of book covers and pointed to one. "*Feline Fury* . . . I loved that one!"

"Let me guess. Possessed cat?"

"Yes. I recently reread it and I swear it could be Blueberry's biography."

Bruce snickered and then pointed at another framed cover. "*Hell Seed*?"

"Possessed baby. That one cost me a lot of money because I stopped babysitting after reading that one my sophomore year of high school."

"You've read every one, haven't you?"

"Some of them twice."

"Sorry to keep you waiting," Shane said gloomily as he descended the stairs. "Unfortunately Mr. Cross is not feeling well so he cannot accept visitors today. He's been working very hard to meet his latest publishing deadline and the stress has sadly taken its toll."

Bruce wasn't ready to give up. "I only have a few questions. I promise it won't take long.

Shane managed a sympathetic smile and then shook his head firmly. "I'm afraid not. Another time."

Bruce was like a dog with a bone. He wasn't going to let it go. "Well, can we come back first thing in the morning? Maybe Mr. Cross will be feeling better by then."

Shane's sympathy was slowly fading and he now appeared slightly annoyed with Bruce's pushy demeanor. "I would appreciate it if you called first instead of just showing up at the door. It would be a shame to come all this way if Mr. Cross is still feeling ill and unable to see you."

"Thank you. You've been very helpful," Hayley said, taking the hint. "Come on, Bruce, let's go."

Hayley knew Bruce's reporter instincts had kicked in and he was questioning this kid's story.

Was Norman Cross really not feeling well?

Or was he purposely dodging having to talk to a couple of nosy newspaper journalists?

And why?

"Wait," Shane said as they were halfway to the door. "I have something for you."

They turned back around to see Shane cross to a desk by the bay window and open a rickety drawer that got stuck halfway. He yanked on the knob several times, swearing to himself, before it was finally open enough for him to get what he was after.

He breezed back over to them and handed them two printed tickets.

"What are these?" Bruce asked, not at all happy about being turned away when he was trying to investigate a story.

"I hate the idea of you coming all the way here for nothing so I thought these might help make it up to you."

"What are they?" Bruce asked.

"Two free passes to the Cross House of Horrors."

The Cross House of Horrors was an annual Halloween tradition started by Norman Cross, who thought it would be fun to transform the abandoned house he owned next door to his mansion into a spooky fright fest complete with moaning ghosts, sticky spider webs, spine-chilling screams, and a host of other carefully orchestrated scary surprises. He even made a habit of hiring local actors from the community theater and high school drama club to dress up as haunting ghouls and murderous maniacs and jump out at you when you least expected.

Every kid in town couldn't wait to go every year during the first week of October when it opened.

Gemma and Dustin had been countless times with their friends.

Hayley had gone once during high school with Mona and Liddy but was so traumatized by the experience she vowed never to go back.

And she didn't.

Once Hayley and Bruce stepped back outside on the porch, Shane slammed the door behind them with a whoosh, obviously grateful to finally be rid of them.

Bruce stared at the two tickets in his hand.

"Don't be frustrated, Bruce. We'll keep checking back in until he's well enough to see us."

"It's not that. I . . ."

"What is it?"

"I've just always wanted to go to the Cross House of Horrors."

"Are you telling me you've *never* gone? Not even when you were a kid?"

"No. My parents never allowed me to go because I had a very weak stomach and they didn't want me throwing up on everybody when I got scared."

Hayley stifled a laugh. "That's perfectly understandable."

"Don't make fun of me," Bruce warned.

"Never. Never," Hayley said, biting the side of her

mouth hard, hoping the concentrated pain would stop her from bursting out into hysterics.

"When I became an adult and could make my own decisions, I didn't think it was a cool thing to do anymore."

"Well, once was enough for me."

"I'd really like to check it off my bucket list."

"Well, first of all, Bruce, the fact that visiting the Cross House of Horrors is actually on your bucket list is scary enough, but I really think you should go."

"We have two free tickets. Don't you want to come with me?"

"Well, gosh, let me think about it . . . No! I barely survived the first time. I was never so scared in my life."

"But you were a kid back then. Come on, you're all grown up now. What are you frightened of?"

"You mean besides my credit card bill? Nothing, I guess."

"So come with me."

"Only if you admit the reason you want me to come with you is because you're too scared to go alone!"

"I will freely admit that. Plus, if I do throw up, you can hold my head."

Chapter 20

Freddy Krueger lunged out of the shadows, grabbing Bruce by the shirtsleeve and causing him to scream like a frightened little girl.

Hayley would have erupted in laughter if not for the fact that Michael Meyers from the *Halloween* movies in that ghostly white mask with the eyes cut out was hovering over her right shoulder.

Bruce squeezed Hayley's hand so tight he cut off the circulation to her fingers. And then he nearly yanked her left arm out of the socket as he dragged her down a darkened hallway away from the cackling Freddy Krueger, who merrily chased behind them.

They rounded a corner and found themselves face to face with Pumpkinhead, who wielded a fake chainsaw.

Or at least Hayley hoped it was fake.

He was pulling on the cord and the deafening roar of the engine caused both her and Bruce to scream at the top of their lungs.

It took her a moment to realize the chainsaw wasn't

real and the sound of it roaring to life was coming from a pair of speakers on the wall.

All of Bruce's false bravado about keeping Hayley safe as they entered past the Styrofoam tombstones planted along the gravel driveway outside leading up to the main door evaporated instantly the minute they actually stepped inside the house.

They struggled through thick, sticky cobwebs and then jumped as a pair of bony white hands grabbed at their legs and arms. They stomped their feet free, screaming, and made their way deeper inside the Cross House of Horrors.

Bruce continued dragging Hayley through the dark, dizzying maze past a dining room filled with carved-up dead bodies seated around the table and then through a parlor populated by a family of decapitated corpses.

A giant spider with red eyes and long, furry, crooked spider legs popped up from the floor with a bloodcurdling scream that did very little to drown out Bruce's own high-pitched squeals of terror.

The shock caused him to finally let go of Hayley's hand.

She shook it hard, trying to get the feeling back in her fingers.

Then Jason from the *Friday the 13th* movies, brandishing a sharp-edged razor, sprung out of a closet.

Bruce screamed bloody murder and grabbed Hayley, fastening her into an iron-tight embrace.

And he wouldn't let go.

"Bruce! Bruce! You're crushing me! I can't breathe!"

She finally managed to extricate herself from Bruce's grip.

"Look, you're disoriented. You keep leading us away from the exit. Now follow me. I think we can get out if we go this way," Hayley screamed, taking charge.

"Just get us the hell out of here! I'm done!" Bruce wailed.

Hayley grabbed him by the shirtsleeve and led him back in the direction from where they had just come.

As they rounded the corner, they found themselves trapped in a pitch-black dead end. Pinhead with the tattooed scalp from the *Hellraiser* movies appeared behind Hayley and grabbed her around the waist lifting her off the floor.

Bruce just stood frozen in place as Hayley noticed the actor, a six-foot-two lumbering kid around college age who they cast to play Pinhead, was obviously enjoying his job a little too much because he was enthusiastically fondling her breasts as they grappled.

Hayley had to slap his hands away until he got a firm message and stopped trying to paw her.

That's when he pushed Hayley to the side and focused his attention on Bruce.

But poor Bruce had been through enough.

He just wanted out.

Spinning around, he tried hightailing it out of there but he slipped on something wet on the floor.

His legs flew out from under him and he landed hard on his back.

He was lying on the floor groaning as Pinhead stepped over him and trotted off to find some more unsuspecting victims.

Hayley scooted over and knelt down by his side. "Bruce, are you okay?"

"I'm all right. I don't think there's anything broken."

As Hayley gingerly tried helping him to his feet, he howled in pain as he made an attempt to stand up. "My back! My back! I think I pulled a muscle or something . . ."

"Okay, take it easy. I'm going to get you out of here."

Hayley put his right arm around her neck and slowly, carefully managed to get him standing on his feet, and then led him through the darkened maze while ignoring the screams and ghostly apparitions projected onto the walls, and swatting away any live actors who tried to slow down their progress with their various surprise scare tactics.

After what seemed like an eternity, Hayley spotted a red exit sign, and after dragging Bruce over to the door, she used her shoulder to shove it open. Then she escorted Bruce down a flight of wooden stairs and out a back door that led to the rear of the abandoned property.

Bruce hobbled over to a tree and leaned against it, moaning and wincing in pain.

"I'm so embarrassed . . ." Bruce whispered.

"Don't be. I was just as scared as you. It's no big deal. How's your back?"

"I think I better go see a doctor. I'm in agony."

"What did you slip on?"

"I don't know. There was something wet and gooey on the floor."

He lifted his foot and examined the sole of his shoe.

It was covered with a green, gelatinous substance.

Hayley raced over and scooped some off his shoe with her finger to examine it more closely.

"This is the same stuff we saw on the bottom of Otis's boot when they found his body in the cemetery," Hayley gasped.

"Which means?"

"Which means he was here before he was killed."

Chapter 21

"Half the town has been to the Cross House of Horrors," Sergio said, stabbing at a generous piece of Hayley's pumpkin cheesecake with his fork. "It's not so unusual that Otis Pearson might go there at some point for punts."

"Punts?" Dustin asked, confused.

"Kicks," Randy said, smiling. "He means Otis might have gone there for kicks."

"Why does everyone insist on correcting me all the time? It's not like you don't understand me!" Sergio barked, wiping some cream cheese off his mustache with his finger and licking it off.

Everyone continued eating their dessert in silence in Hayley's dining room, choosing to let the moment float by without further comment.

Finally, after scraping the last bits of cheesecake off her plate with her fork, Hayley said, "Well, I, for one, think it's rather strange that Otis went to make a moonshine delivery to Norman Cross on the night he died, and then somehow mysteriously ended up next door at the Cross House of Horrors where he picked up that green goo on the bottom of his boot, and then later was found dead in the cemetery. The only person who may be able to shine some light on what really happened is Norman Cross."

"Are you saying Cross might have had something to do with Otis's murder?" Randy asked, sipping a glass of Chardonnay.

"No. I honestly don't know what I'm saying. None of this makes any sense," Hayley said, frustrated.

Dustin perked up. "Hey! I know what happened! Maybe Otis decided to go to the House of Horrors after his delivery and it was there that one of the actors playing a serial killer got a little too into his role and bopped him over the head by accident or something! Then he panicked after realizing what he had done and so he dragged Otis's body to the cemetery to fool the police into thinking he was killed there!"

"That's not a bad theory," Sergio admitted before wiping his mouth with a napkin. "I've got a list of the actors employed by Norman Cross at the House of Horrors so I'm going to question them all thoroughly tomorrow."

Dustin grinned from ear to ear, proud of himself for coming up with a plausible solution to the crime.

The front door burst open and Danny breezed in, looking a bit harried. "Sorry I missed dinner. I got tied up."

"That's okay, because I never invited you," Hayley remarked, standing up to clear the dessert plates off the table.

"I invited him, Mom," Gemma said.

Danny spotted the half-eaten cheesecake in the middle of the table. He scooped up a knife and cut himself a generous piece before plopping down in Hayley's vacant chair to chow down.

Randy jumped up from the table. "Can I make you a drink, Danny?"

Danny took Randy's hand and squeezed it. "You spoil me, Randy-boy."

Randy giggled and blushed.

Sergio raised an eyebrow.

Gemma and Dustin tried hard not to laugh.

"How about a whiskey and soda?" Danny said, winking.

"Coming right up," Randy said, bumping into a chair as he smiled and backed out of the room.

Sergio watched him go, fascinated.

As if he could not believe Randy was susceptible to this two-bit con artist's charms.

Hayley stacked the dirty plates, picked them up, and followed Randy into the kitchen where they could still overhear the conversation going on in the dining room.

"So what are we talking about?" Danny asked with a mouthful of cheesecake.

"Otis Pearson's murder," Sergio said, sitting back in his chair and glaring at him.

"Not exactly my first choice for dinner conversation," Danny said.

"Dinner's over," Hayley said, returning to the table after depositing the dirty dishes in the sink.

"Any suspects, Chief?" Danny asked casually.

Sergio never took his eyes off Danny, working

hard to intimidate him. "I have a few persons of interest."

Danny nodded and cracked a half smile. "Well, with any luck, you'll find the piece of crap who knocked off poor old Uncle Otis and we can finally be done with all this messy business."

"I will. Believe me," Sergio said quietly and forcefully enough to cause Danny to shift in his seat uncomfortably.

"A bit cold in here, isn't it, Hayley? Want me to start a fire?" Danny said in an effort to change the subject.

"I'm perfectly comfortable, but thank you, Danny," Hayley said.

"Really? Nobody else is a little chilly?"

The kids shook their heads.

Sergio just shrugged and gave him a look that said, *You're on your own, buddy*.

Randy appeared with a cocktail and set it down in front of Danny.

"Thank you, handsome," Danny said, and then gulped down his drink to avoid any further discussion about his uncle Otis.

"Well, this has been fun but I have a long day ahead tomorrow," Sergio said, signaling Randy that it was time to hit the road.

Hayley wrapped the leftover cheesecake in Saran Wrap and put it in the refrigerator as Randy and Sergio gave the kids hugs good night. Then Hayley led them to the door and gave them both kisses on the cheek.

"I'll call you tomorrow," Randy said before following Sergio to the car.

As they drove away, Hayley stood in the doorway watching them go.

Danny sauntered up behind her and put his cold hands on her warm shoulders.

Her body shook slightly from his touch.

"See? You *are* cold," Danny said, leaning forward and whispering in her ear.

"No. Your hands are cold."

He rubbed her shoulders.

She fought the urge to lean her head back and rest it on his chest like she used to do.

That's when she noticed a sedan, a Toyota Camry or a similar model, parked across the street.

The lights were off but she could see the silhouettes of two men sitting in the front seats.

"Danny, look. Who are those guys?"

Danny squinted to get a good look at them, but then shook his head dismissively.

"Beats me."

"Why are they just sitting there?"

"Maybe they're on a date."

Hayley gave him a skeptical look. "It looks like they're watching the house."

"You're being paranoid, babe. It's nothing. And trust me. I've never seen those guys before. Come on, let's go watch TV with the kids," he said, spinning around and disappearing back inside the house.

Hayley wanted to believe him.

She really did.

But how could he know for sure that he didn't know those men who appeared to be staking out her house from across the street?

There was no way he could possibly see their faces in the dark.

The car was parked away from the streetlight in the shadows.

Unless he was lying to her.

Again.

Chapter 22

Hayley immediately spotted the slinky blonde in the tight baby blue sweater, even tighter jeans, and furry tan boots sitting on top of a stool at the far end of the bar when she walked through the door of Drinks Like A Fish.

Randy had called her at work earlier to let her know a young woman in her mid-twenties had shown up at his bar asking all kinds of questions about Hayley.

She inspected the girl who was sipping on a cosmopolitan and ignoring the stares of a group of fishermen at a table behind her ogling her perky breasts and round butt and long, wavy blond hair.

Randy raced out of the kitchen through the revolving doors with a steaming plate of fried clams and set it down in front of the girl, whose eyes widened with delight.

"Do you have tartar sauce?"

"Coming right up," Randy said, catching Hayley out of the corner of his eye and signaling that this was the woman who seemed to be so curious about her.

Hayley gave her another once-over but couldn't place her.

She had no idea who this voluptuous young woman was.

The woman picked up a fried clam and blew on it with her luscious ruby red lips as the fishermen behind her froze in place watching her gently slip the clam into her mouth.

She was slowly chewing it, moaning with ecstasy over the taste when she looked up and saw Hayley taking a seat on the empty stool next to her.

"Hayley? Hayley Powell?"

Hayley pretended it was sheer coincidence that she had just strolled into the bar at that moment, and that her brother had not called her to hightail it over there just as soon as she could to see if she was familiar with this buxom girl who was so curious about her.

"Yes, I'm Hayley. And you are . . . ?"

"Becky . . ."

The name didn't ring a bell at first.

But then, when she repeated the name to herself, it suddenly dawned on her who it was that was sitting right in front of her.

"Becky?"

"Yes. Becky Cameron," she said with a bright smile.

This was Danny's Becky.

His wispy, IQ-deprived sexpot of a girlfriend for the past two and a half years.

Here in Bar Harbor.

"You're much prettier in person," Becky said, studying Hayley's face. "The pictures Danny has of you don't do you justice."

The way Becky said it made it seem like this was bad news. She obviously had a much dowdier image of Hayley in her mind and she was clearly disappointed that Hayley actually surpassed her first impression.

"What brings you to town, Becky?"

"Really? Do you honestly not know? I'm here to see Danny. He is still here, isn't he?"

"Oh, yes. He's not allowed to go anywhere."

Becky grimaced. "I see. What kind of trouble has he gotten himself into this time?"

"I better let Danny explain. I was sorry to hear about you two breaking up. Sometimes Danny can be a bit challenged in the commitment department."

"What are you talking about?"

"Well, he told me he ended your relationship before he came here to see the kids."

"Is *that* what he told you?" Becky sneered, before picking up another fried clam and taking a big bite, oblivious to the enraptured fishermen sitting directly behind her nudging each other like rascally schoolboys. "Well, just to set the record straight, Hayley. Danny didn't dump me. I was the one who broke it off with him."

"I'm sorry. He told me . . ."

"I'm sure he said anything in order to avoid looking like the lame loser who lost the best thing that ever happened to him, but facts are facts."

Hayley nodded, having no intention of arguing with Becky. "Okay. So where are you staying while you're in town?"

"I booked a room at a quiet little motel just outside of town. It has a fireplace!"

"How long will you be in Bar Harbor?"

Becky shrugged. "I haven't thought that far ahead yet. I booked a one-way ticket. I just had to get here as soon as possible."

"It sounds like you're a woman on a mission."

"I am, Hayley. I'm here to take Danny back."

"Oh. So I guess you've forgiven him for . . . whatever it is he did to cause you to break up with him?"

"Yes. I had this romantic notion of being a single girl again and going out with my friends and letting cute guys buy me drinks like in the good old days . . . but the reality wasn't close to what I thought it was going to be like, and those cute guys aren't so cute when they're drunk and horny. So I thought it was time I gave Danny one more chance."

Hayley signaled Randy to bring her a Jack and Coke.

Becky stared at her for a long moment, making her supremely uncomfortable before saying, "I certainly hope Danny coming back here to see his children wasn't misconstrued or anything . . ."

"What do you mean?"

"I mean you're not hoping you and Danny are going to get back together, are you? I really want us to be close gal pals, Hayley. But if you have designs on Danny, that's really going to squash our blossoming friendship."

Hayley burst out laughing. "Designs on Danny . . . ? No . . . No, Becky . . . you have nothing to worry about . . ."

"What's so funny?"

"Just that you thought I was still interested in Danny and the idea of that is just so . . . so . . . crazy."

"Why is that so crazy? You married him once."

"Yes. And that's why it's so crazy. I would never make the same mistake twice. Especially a mistake that big!"

"Do you think I'm a fool for loving him? For giving him another chance to make me happy?"

Randy delivered the Jack and Coke, and Hayley gulped it down to give herself the strength to make it through this land mine–filled conversation.

"Absolutely not. Danny and I were like oil and water. But you two seem to complement each other," Hayley blurted out, backpedaling as fast as she could. "It's an entirely different situation. But I want to assure you, Becky, and I am being one hundred percent honest here, I am *not* a threat to you. I have no interest in rekindling anything with Danny. He's all yours. Totally. I will never, ever, ever stand in the way of your relationship with him. I mean that with all my heart."

Becky stared at her for almost a minute.

Hayley was confident she had finally gotten through to her.

But then, Becky said offhandedly, "I don't believe you."

Hayley waved at Randy to bring her another Jack and Coke.

Pronto.

She was going to need it.

The door to the bar flew open and Danny plowed inside, panic-stricken. He took a deep breath at the sight of Hayley and Becky sitting side by side at the bar chatting away, and then marched over to them, plastering a big wide smile on his face.

"Becky, sweet pea, what are you doing here? I

couldn't believe it when you texted me and said you were in town."

Becky smiled like a Cheshire cat, grabbed his hand, and brushed it along the side of her cheek warmly. "I've missed you."

She batted her eyes at him.

The fishermen watching melted.

They all pictured themselves as Danny getting stroked on the face by a hot, gorgeous blonde.

Danny just stood there awkwardly as she took his hand and kissed his fingers.

One.

Two.

Three.

Four.

And last but not least the pinkie.

"Hayley's been so sweet keeping me company until you showed up," she said tracing the lifeline on the palm of his hand.

Danny slowly removed his hand and kissed her lightly on the cheek.

"Yes. She's been telling me all about how things ended between you two," Hayley said pointedly.

Danny nodded, caught. "I need a beer."

He waved at Randy, who went to the cooler for a bottle and brought it over to him.

Danny cleared his throat. "I guess she must have told you that I wasn't the one who ended things."

"Yes, she may have mentioned that in passing," Hayley said evenly.

"I didn't want you to think I had nowhere to go, and so that's why I came crawling back here. I wanted you to think I was in a good place, in charge of my life, had my act together."

"Why, Danny? Why couldn't you just be up-front with me?" Hayley asked, exhausted from trying to decipher her husband's doublespeak.

"Because I want you back, Hayley," Danny said.

It seemed to have just slipped out.

And as soon as the words rolled off his tongue, Danny sucked in air, hoping to pull them all back, but it was too late.

Becky's whole body tensed as she twisted around and stared at him. "*What* did you just say?"

"I . . . I still love her, Becky . . ."

Hayley wanted to bolt out the door.

But she was afraid to make any kind of sudden move.

"But I came all the way here to take you back . . . You can't do this to me . . ." Becky cried, quickly unraveling.

One fisherman at the table behind her pushed his chair back as if he was getting ready to take on the role of Prince Charming and swoop in to save this desperate damsel in distress, but his buddies quietly reminded him he smelled of fish bait and beer breath so he decided to stay put.

Becky slowly turned her head, her eyes boring into Hayley, who shuddered and winced.

"Seriously, I . . . I had no idea . . ." Hayley sputtered. "Really . . . What I told you is the truth . . . I have no intention of ever taking him back . . ."

Before she could finish, Becky picked up the plate of fried clams and hurled them at Danny, who ducked. The plate smashed on the floor, the fried clams scattering everywhere.

Then she went berserk, picking up bottles and glasses and throwing them everywhere.

The fishermen ducked underneath their table to avoid all the flying glass.

Randy raced out from behind the bar screaming at Becky, "Get out! Get out of my bar right now before I call the police!"

But Becky was in the zone.

There was no speaking to her rationally.

She was hell-bent on destroying everything in her path, upending tables and smashing beer mugs on the floor.

Randy plucked his cell phone out of the back pocket of his jeans and punched in 911.

Danny grabbed Hayley by the hand and yanked her toward the door.

"Come on, let's get the hell out of here before she kills us!"

Chapter 23

Hayley and Danny tore out of Drinks Like A Fish and dashed across the street to Danny's rental car. As Danny fumbled for the keys in his pocket, Hayley spotted Becky flying out of the bar behind them, a crazed look on her face, screaming, "Danny, get back here right now!"

Danny had no intention of facing her wrath.

He was done.

He pressed the unlock button on the remote and there was a click.

Hayley and Danny jumped in the car just as Becky charged across the street nearly getting mowed down by seventy-six-year-old Mabel Forrester in her Buick Skylark who was heading toward the Shop 'n Save to buy her week's worth of groceries. Mabel slammed on the brakes and screeched to a stop in the middle of the street as Becky slammed her fists down on the hood of the car.

"Watch where you're going, you old bat!" Becky shrieked.

Mabel just sat frozen behind the wheel, shaken by the close call.

The distraction gave Danny the precious time he needed to start the engine and back out of his parking space.

The tires squealed as they sped off down the street, but not before Becky furiously hurled her purse at them.

Hayley glanced at the rearview mirror in time to see it bounce off the back windshield and land on the pavement, the contents flying out in all different directions.

Becky didn't bother retrieving her belongings.

Except for her car keys, which she scooped up in her hand as she ran to her own rental car, a gray Nissan Versa, and hopped in the driver's seat.

Hayley cranked her head around and watched in horror as Becky chased after them in hot pursuit, gripping the steering wheel, wild-eyed with fury.

"She's closing in on us, Danny!" Hayley screamed.

"What the—? You have got to be kidding me!" Danny yelled, cranking his head around to see her coming up behind them before turning back to keep his eyes fixed on the road. "Sometimes when she loses her head, there's no reasoning with her."

"Yeah, I got that impression," Hayley said, turning back around and checking to make sure her seatbelt was securely fastened.

Danny yanked the wheel sharply to the right as they zipped past a stop sign and squealed onto Route 3, which led them out of town.

"Danny, slow down! You're going to get us killed!"

"You don't know Becky! There's no telling what she'll do if she catches up to us!"

"What do you mean? Just how crazy is she?"

Before Danny had a chance to answer, something slammed into the back of their car and they were thrown forward. The strap of the locked seatbelts jerked them back into their seats and the back of Hayley's head banged against the headrest hard.

"What the hell is she doing?" Hayley cried, whipping around to see Becky in her car, bumper to bumper, screaming expletives that they thankfully couldn't hear.

"Oh dear God, she's trying to kill us!"

"No, she's just trying to get us to pull over!"

"Well, do it, Danny, before she sends us hurtling over a cliff!"

"It's too risky! She may have her gun on her and she's not thinking clearly right now!"

"She owns a *gun*?"

"Fifteen of them. Proud card-carrying member of the NRA since the age of eighteen!"

"I can't believe my life is going to end at the hands of your crazy girlfriend Annie Oakley!"

"*Ex*-girlfriend!"

"I don't care, Danny! It doesn't matter! You're the reason she's trying to kill us!"

Danny suddenly swerved the car to the left in order to get them off the main road and they raced past the entrance to Acadia National Park, which had less traffic this time of year.

But he missed the sharp turn and the rental car spun out of control and flew off the road. It landed in a ditch and crushed the whole front end of the car.

Hayley and Danny sat in silence for a moment

staring out the cracked windshield, both in a state of shock.

Hayley finally found her voice. "I sure hope you have insurance."

They heard the Nissan Versa screech to a stop back up on the paved road and a car door open and slam shut.

"Danny? Are you all right? Are you still alive?" Becky hollered. "Should I call an ambulance? Answer me, Danny!"

"Don't move a muscle. If she thinks we're dead, she might panic and get back in her car and drive away," Danny whispered urgently.

Hayley couldn't believe this was happening.

She was lying in a totaled car in a muddy ditch pretending she was dead so as not to be shot in the head by her ex-husband's psycho sweetheart.

"Danny?" Becky barked. "You better not be playing games with me!"

Smoke billowed out from under the mangled hood of Danny's rental.

"What if the car catches on fire?" Hayley frantically whispered.

"Better to be burned alive then get out of this car and have to face *her*," Danny muttered.

Hayley held her breath as she heard Becky climbing down the embankment and into the ditch making her way to the car.

Hayley popped one eye open to steal a glance through the rearview mirror.

Becky didn't appear to be carrying a gun.

Suddenly they heard sirens.

A squad car skidded to a stop behind Becky's vehicle.

Officers Donnie and Earl, Sergio's trustworthy although not always competent deputies, appeared at the roadside as they peered down at the wreckage.

"What happened?" she heard Earl call down.

"My fiancé lost control of his vehicle and ended up down in this ditch!" Becky yelled back.

Fiancé?

Danny may have lost control of his rental car but Becky had obviously lost control of reality.

Hayley shoved the passenger's side door open and crawled out of the car. "We're okay, boys! Nobody got hurt!"

Donnie and Earl exchanged a quick look.

Neither was surprised that Hayley Powell was somehow involved in this mess.

It rankled her that they would think that, but on the other hand, she had given them plenty of reasons over the years to give them just cause.

Donnie turned to Earl. "I'm going to call a tow truck. You take their statements."

"Roger that," Earl said, relishing the use of official cop talk.

Donnie trotted back to the squad car as Earl, who was short and pudgy and not all that agile, tried to make his way down the embankment. He lost his footing and toppled over, sliding all the way down on his butt.

Becky stifled a laugh.

"Are you hurt, Earl?" Hayley asked.

"Just my pride," Earl mumbled.

"Danny, the car looks pretty totaled," Hayley said.

"You better call the rental company and have them send you another one."

"My car insurance doesn't carry over to the rental! Which means they're going to charge my credit card on file for the damages, and it's already close to the limit!" Danny moaned. "I just can't catch a break!"

"Let's just be happy we're alive, okay?" Hayley said, shaking her head.

"None of this would have happened if you had just pulled over," Becky said, annoyed. "I mean, all I wanted was for the three of us to have a reasonable adult conversation."

"Reasonable conversation? You chased us out of the bar! You rear-ended us with your car! You're the reason we ended up in this ditch!" Hayley screamed.

"Actually, if truth be told, that was Danny. He took that turn way too fast. I've been telling him he should be more careful behind the wheel," Becky said defensively.

"Wait a minute, lady," Earl said, perking up. "You purposely rammed them with your car?"

"I may have bumped them just a bit but it was only because they wouldn't stop and I really needed to talk to them," Becky said, completely convinced she was in the right.

"That's reckless endangerment," Earl said.

"Such big words for such a simple boy," Becky sneered.

She was not willing to take the situation seriously.

Earl reached for his handcuffs. "I'm placing you under arrest, lady!"

Becky backed away. "Oh, no you're not. Don't be silly."

Earl tried to slip an open handcuff around her wrist, but she slapped it away.

"You want me to add resisting arrest to the charges?" Earl warned, putting on his best badass serious cop face.

Becky sighed, resigned, and held out her hands. "You're going to regret this, little boy blue."

Danny was suddenly distracted by the trunk of the car, which was damaged enough it popped open.

He raced over to slam it shut.

But it wouldn't stay down.

It kept popping up again.

"Danny, just leave it . . . ." Hayley said. "The car's wrecked beyond repair."

But he wouldn't listen.

He continued shutting it again and again, leaning against it, almost climbing on top to sit on it.

Finally, Hayley walked over as he desperately tried holding the trunk lid shut and physically pulled him away. "It's busted, Danny. Get over it."

Danny's hand slipped away as she pulled on his sleeve and the trunk lid flew wide open.

That's when Hayley saw a couple of large green plastic garbage bags torn open and wads of cash strewn all over the inside of the trunk.

"Danny . . . ?" Hayley gasped.

There had to be at least thirty or forty thousand dollars in there.

Earl, who had finally securely fastened the handcuffs on Becky's wrists behind her back, led her over and they all stared inside at the huge pile of money.

"Danny, please don't tell me . . ." Hayley said, her voice trailing off.

Danny looked away.

It was Otis Pearson's missing savings.

Forty thousand dollars.

Despite her desperately wanting to give him the benefit of the doubt, Hayley knew Danny had stolen it.

And that Becky wasn't the only one who was going to be arrested that day.

Only Danny's charges were destined to be far more serious.

He was going to have to answer for theft and suspicion of murder.

Island Food & Spirits
by
Hayley Powell

A heaping serving of my delicious
Pumpkin Stew is guaranteed to wash
away all of life's problems. With each
spoonful, I promise you will feel weeks
of tension slowly draining from your
body. That's what happened to me last
night. Until my son walked in the
kitchen and said the words every
mother dreads hearing from her child.

"Mom, I want to sign up for Driver's
Education next semester!"

What?

How on earth was he fifteen years
old already?

Why hadn't I seen this coming?

I turned to my daughter, who was a
few years older than her brother and
quietly eating a bowl of my Pumpkin
Stew, and all of the traumatic, horrify-
ing memories of her learning to drive
came flooding back to me.

Let's just say neither of us appealed to the better angels of our nature during that trying time. And reliving those moments required me to fish out another pumpkin-inspired treat out of my plastic recipe box, my special Pumpkin Pie Cocktail, which I was counting on to go a long way in calming my nerves.

It seemed just like yesterday when Gemma turned fifteen and was ready to study for her driver's permit, an island tradition that dates back to the invention of the automobile when teenagers all over the area dreamed of having that coveted driver's license and the imagined freedom that goes along with it. Like driving off the island without your parents to the big city of Ellsworth, a magical land with shopping malls and fast-food chains. Or if they were really lucky, they might get all the way to Bangor with its bright lights and movie multiplexes and even bigger shopping malls with store names you've actually heard before!

I remember when my time came I was pretty darn excited. And now with my daughter on the cusp of that independence I couldn't have been happier. Finally, my daughter could drive to the store when we needed toilet paper or a bag of flour. She could fetch her brother after school, or even, although

I shouldn't admit this, pick up me and my BFFs after a night on the town. Okay, let's scratch that one and forget I ever said it.

The best bonus, however, was the mother-and-daughter bonding time we could share while I took her out to practice her driving. The last person a fifteen-year-old girl wants to hang out with is her mother, but now we would have hours of time together while navigating turns and perfecting her parallel parking skills.

It didn't quite work out that way when she was finally awarded her permit. Our first drive together to the Trenton Bridge and back didn't exactly foster a bond. How could it with me pumping my feet up and down on the floorboard, screaming for her to slow down every two minutes? Or pointing out a rogue squirrel darting across the road ahead? Or grabbing the steering wheel twice and yanking it too hard to the left when I thought she was drifting across the center line?

The final straw was when we arrived in our driveway and I jumped from the car and got down on my knees and kissed the pavement. It was meant to be a little joke. But any hopes of bonding at that point were dashed. My daughter was furious.

I was ashamed of myself. I was supposed to be the "cool mom," the one who welcomed my kid taking over the wheel during a family road trip, who loved riding shotgun with her daughter. That's who I wanted to be. So I apologized for my frayed nerves that day, chalking it up to all the day's excitement over her finally getting her permit, and begged for another chance. Thankfully she agreed.

The next morning, we tried again. Everything was fine until my daughter turned the ignition key. As the engine roared to life, I felt my stomach twist into a knot. A small bubble of panic began rising until my heart was beating twice as fast as usual.

Breathe.

Breathe.

She put the car in reverse and began backing out of the driveway. That's when I heard myself screaming, "You're too close to the lawn! Stay on the pavement! Did you even look in your rearview mirror? There's a dog in the street!"

Gemma yelled back, "I'm not even close to the lawn! Yes, I looked in the mirror! And the dog is on his own property nowhere near the street!"

It was as if I was outside my body watching this awful woman overreacting to everything.

"If you were just twelve more inches over on my side you'd be on the lawn!"

At that point, my daughter turned off the car, jumped out, and ran crying into the house wailing, "I will never drive with you again!"

Actually she did.

We tried four more times.

And we never left the driveway.

One of us would inevitably get out of the car and storm inside the house. I had to take a good look at myself and admit that I was never going to be able to ride with my daughter without turning into this shrill, panicky, obnoxious, overbearing mother. Her words, not mine.

It was time to call in the cavalry. If my daughter was ever going to be prepared for her official driver's test, she needed someone calm and understanding in the passenger's seat. That turned out to be my brother, Randy. They formed the special bond I dreamed about. And she sailed through her test with flying colors. I'm sure I will get comfortable with the idea of her driving me around soon . . . like when she turns thirty.

As for my son, his uncle Sergio has signed up for driving duty to get him prepared for his own test. We all agree I should just stay out of it. They say the definition of insanity is repeating the same action over and over expecting a different outcome. So I will not be getting in a car with one of my children anytime soon.

Pumpkin Stew

<u>Ingredients</u>
½ cup flour
½ teaspoon salt
½ teaspoon pepper
2 pounds stew meat cut into one-inch
 cubes
2 tablespoons canola oil
2 tablespoons butter
1 large onion, chopped
2 to 3 cloves garlic, chopped
3 carrots, thinly sliced
2 celery ribs, thinly sliced
4 cups veggie broth or you can use
 water
1 bay leaf
2 teaspoons beef bouillon granules
3 cups peeled and cubed pumpkin

Using a large resealable plastic bag add your flour, salt, pepper. Then add your cubed stew meat a few pieces at a time and shake to coat, remove, and put on a plate until all pieces are coated.

In your Dutch oven or large heavy pot add your oil and butter until heated. Add your meat and let it brown a bit.

Add your onion and garlic, and cook for about 3 minutes (do not burn garlic). Stir in the carrots and celery, broth (water), bay leaf, and bullion. Cover and simmer for 1½ hours.

Stir in pumpkin and bring to a boil, then reduce heat; cover and simmer for 30 minutes or until pumpkin and meat are tender. Discard your bay leaf.

Ladle into soup bowls and serve with some crusty bread and enjoy.

Pumpkin Pie Cocktail

Ingredients

1 ounce coconut rum
½ ounce Kahlúa
¾ ounce pumpkin pie filling
2 ounces milk
Crushed graham crackers

Add the rum, Kahlúa, pie filling, and milk in a cocktail shaker filled with ice and shake well. Serve in an ice-filled glass rimmed with crushed graham crackers. This is the kind of spirit I want to conjure up on Halloween!

Chapter 24

"See, babe? You just have to have a little faith. I'm in the clear," Danny crowed before munching down on a big hunk of green apple he had taken from a wooden bowl in Hayley's kitchen.

He was right.

Danny had breezed through the door in high spirits five minutes earlier after Sergio released him from jail.

The coroner had issued his official report and had been able to narrow down Otis Pearson's time of death. He died from a severe blow to the head by a blunt object between the hours of seven and nine in the evening. That was during the time Danny was chowing down on pizza and treating Hayley and the kids to a movie before he decided he wanted to leave and ushered them all out.

Still, he remained with them until well past nine.

It would have been impossible for him to have driven to Tremont and kill his uncle Otis during that time.

"I think this is cause for a celebration!" Danny

DEATH OF A PUMPKIN CARVER   177

said, jubilant and full of bluster and swagger over once again avoiding a disaster. "How about Bella Vita? They're still open until Thanksgiving, right? I'm thinking a nice bottle of Cabernet, a hearty plate of linguini with clam sauce? Some tiramisu? Just you, me, and the kids. Sound good?"

"Wait, Danny . . ."

He wasn't listening. He was already in the hallway yelling up the stairs to the kids. "Gemma! Dustin! Come on down here and bring your appetites! I'm taking us out to dinner!"

"Danny, just hold on a minute! You may be innocent of murder but what about the theft?"

"I'm sure Sergio will see to it that whole thing goes away. After all, I'm family," Danny said confidently, grabbing his coat off the back of one of Hayley's high-back kitchen chairs.

"You're not family. Anymore. And I'm fairly certain Sergio won't just forget about it. How are you even out of jail if you're still facing the theft charge?"

"I posted bail. It was only five hundred dollars," Danny said, grinning from ear to ear. "I happened to have some money in my wallet. With enough to spare for dinner tonight."

"That's Uncle Otis's money, isn't it? It wasn't all in the trunk. You had already stuffed some bills in your wallet, am I right, Danny?"

He winked at her. "I'll neither confirm nor deny."

"Oh, Danny," Hayley moaned, shaking her head. "And what about Becky?"

"What about her?"

"She's still in jail!"

"Yeah, so? I wasn't about to bail her out too just so she could try to kill us again," Danny said, shrugging.

He had a point.

"Don't worry about Becky. Her father's wiring her some money. She'll be out by morning, okay?" Danny said.

They could hear the kids coming out of their rooms.

Danny leaned in and spoke in a low voice so the kids couldn't hear him as they bounded down the stairs. "Look, I admit I took the money but it was mine to take. Uncle Otis told me that if anything ever happened to him, that money was mine. He *wanted* me to have it."

Hayley gave him a skeptical look as Gemma and Dustin ambled into the kitchen.

"What did you do, Dad? Bust out of jail?" Dustin asked, chuckling.

"I'm a law-abiding citizen, Dustin. I would never break the law because that would set a bad example for my two adorable children."

Gemma hugged her father. "I'm glad you're out. I was worried about you, Dad."

"I wish you could've stayed in jail just a little while longer. Having a dad behind bars was making me cooler to the other kids at school. You should see all the sympathetic messages I've been getting just in the last hour from a bunch of hot girls on Facebook."

"I don't know what's sadder. Using our father's incarceration to impress girls or the fact you still use Facebook," Gemma said.

"Okay, everybody pile into the car. Dad's treating

the family to dinner tonight," Danny said, leading the way.

Hayley cringed.

She didn't like him talking as if they were still a tight-knit family unit.

She didn't want the kids getting a false impression.

That it was in the realm of possibility they might somehow get back together.

Because that was never going to happen.

"With what, Dad? I thought Uncle Sergio confiscated the stolen money," Dustin said.

"Would everybody stop saying the word 'stolen'? I didn't *steal* anything!"

Just before Danny could herd everyone out the back door to the driveway, there was a loud banging on the front door.

"Gemma, go see who it is," Hayley said.

Gemma sighed and marched back through the kitchen, down the hall, and out onto the front patio to open the door.

Spanky McFarland, Dustin's aspiring writer and best buddy, flew past her with a whoosh and raced into the kitchen.

His face was dripping with sweat, his cheeks were red, and he was hyperventilating to the point where he had to fish an inhaler out of his pants pocket and take a hit.

"Spanky, what's wrong? What happened?" Dustin asked as they all waited patiently for him to catch his breath.

He tried to speak.

But then he began hyperventilating again.

He shoved the inhaler back in his mouth.

"Good Lord, calm down, Spanky," Hayley said, patting him gently on the back. "Just breathe and relax."

Spanky did as he was told and finally managed to inhale and exhale normally.

"I just came . . . I just came from Norman Cross's house . . ." Spanky sputtered.

He waited for a reaction but didn't get the euphoric cheers he had expected so he continued. "I've been trying to get Mr. Cross to read my horror novel *The Devil's Honeymoon* and I was finally able to get his assistant, Shane, who is a super-nice guy by the way, to invite me over so I could meet him in person and ask him to read my manuscript!"

"Dude, that's awesome!" Dustin shouted, slapping his friend on the back.

"But when I got there Shane told me he was too ill to see me," Spanky said, wiping his nose with his shirtsleeve.

"Sounds familiar," Hayley said. "He must be down with the flu. It's going around."

"I'm hoping there's a silver lining somewhere because you looked really happy and excited when you got here and I hope we get to it soon because I'm hungry," Gemma said, a little impatient.

"Yes, there is!" Spanky cried before reaching back into his pocket for his inhaler. "Wait. Hold on a second."

He took another hit.

Calmed himself down.

And was off and running again.

"Shane told me he talked to Mr. Cross and Mr. Cross said he was going to read my novel and let me know what he thinks! Shane even said if he liked it he just might pass it along to his book publisher!" Spanky screamed, jumping up and down.

Dustin grabbed his buddy in a bear hug and lifted him off the ground as the two boys whooped and hollered with glee.

"Congratulations, Spanky! Now we have two reasons to celebrate. Call your mother and tell her you won't be home for dinner tonight! You're going to eat with us. My treat!" Danny said, rustling the hair on top of Spanky's head with his hand.

"Thank you, Mr. Powell! That's real nice of you!" Spanky said, beaming.

"Blood money," Hayley whispered under her breath as she passed Danny and marched out the back door to the car.

Chapter 25

The next day was the annual Bar Harbor Halloween parade where all the schoolchildren from kindergarten all the way up to the eighth grade marched down Main Street showing off their Halloween costumes.

This year there was a wide variety of ensembles from store-bought outfits to lavishly homemade ones. Lots of superheroes and cartoon characters like Green Lantern, Superman, Batman, Bart Simpson, SpongeBob SquarePants, and Dora the Explorer. Others more unique like four brothers wearing beards made of mops and going as the *Duck Dynasty* brood and three kids in lobster costumes made of felt crowded into a giant steel pot on wheels and being pushed by another boy with a drawn-on goatee, fake tattoos on his arm, and spiked hair pretending to be celebrity chef Guy Fieri. Hayley's favorite were two first graders, a boy and a girl, in black T-shirts and leather pants wearing too much hair gel as Danny and Sandy from *Grease*.

The parade started promptly at three thirty in the

afternoon when it was still light out, allowing the high school kids enough time after their last class to come and watch.

Danny had shown up at the office insisting Hayley accompany him, and despite her initial refusal, Sal once again failed to back up her decision and said in front of Danny that he was fine with her leaving work early to see the parade.

So here she was weaving through the crowd with her ex-husband, who was in a buoyant mood. He clasped her hand so they didn't get separated.

Danny spotted a small opening in the mob of locals clogging the sidewalks and pushed his way forward dragging Hayley behind him until they had jostled their way to a clear view of the parade.

Dustin joined them after getting dropped off by the school bus a few blocks away, and after the first wave of kids started marching down Main Street in their various getups, Gemma texted Hayley to tell her Dr. Aaron had closed the practice early today so the staff could attend. Hayley texted their exact location and Gemma caught up with them a few minutes later.

Danny threw his arms around his kids and pulled them close. "This is so special!"

He squeezed them hard until they both started giggling.

"Like old times. Watching the Halloween parade. As a family . . ." Danny said, his voice trailing off, lost in his memories of years long past.

"Don't get all sentimental, Danny," Hayley said, refusing to allow him to revel too much in his longing for the days when they were still married.

"I think it's sweet, Dad," Gemma said.

"Thank you, baby doll," Danny said, drawing her into his chest so he could kiss the top of her head. "At least you didn't inherit your mother's cynicism."

Hayley ignored the comment and continued watching the parade.

An eighth grader passed by dressed as Optimus Pint, basically a Transformer made of beer cans and cartons.

Hayley didn't want to know where he got the materials.

He was followed by a gaggle of yellow Minions.

A boy dressed as Dr. Evil from the *Austin Powers* movies.

Six seventh-grade girls singing Spanish love songs dressed as a mariachi band.

The costumes seemed to get more clever with each passing year.

"Hey, I just got a text from Spanky," Dustin said, eyeing his phone. "He's at the ice cream shop across from the Village Green and they're offering two-for-one ice cream cones today if you get one of their Halloween flavors like pumpkin spice or candy corn."

"I'm so in. Come on, I'll buy," Gemma said, starting to head off.

"Wait," Danny said, grabbing her sweater to stop her while reaching in his back pocket for his wallet. "I don't want you spending your own money."

"It's fine, Dad. I'm a working girl now," Gemma said.

He pressed a twenty-dollar bill in the palm of her hand. "You save your money for your college expenses. I'll cover this."

Gemma crumpled the money in her hand. "I'll bring you back the change."

"No, you keep it and split it with your brother," Danny said.

"If you keep letting us keep the change, pretty soon I'll be able to raise the whole budget of my first feature film," Dustin said, perking up. "Thanks, Dad."

"Thank his uncle Otis," Hayley said.

She couldn't help herself.

Danny flashed her an irritated look, but he wasn't about to pick a fight.

Gemma and Dustin disappeared into the crowd of spectators.

Danny watched the parade for a few minutes in silence, but it was clear he was bugged by something.

Finally, he spun around to face Hayley.

"I'd really appreciate it if you stopped putting me down in front of my kids."

Hayley was flabbergasted.

"Putting you down? I'm just stating the truth. They're old enough to hear it," Hayley said. "The money you gave them belonged to your uncle Otis."

"And now it belongs to me. How many times do I have to tell you it's what he wanted? And once that's cleared up you'll be apologizing for thinking I plundered from my own family!"

"How are you going to clear it up, Danny? Otis left no will. He never mentioned his wishes to anyone but you while you were both hanging out drinking. And frankly your past history doesn't really instill a lot of confidence in people to give you the benefit of the doubt."

"You never believed in me," Danny said, genuinely hurt.

"Yes, I did, Danny. Time and time again. Even when you'd gamble away our rent money or surprise the kids with a trip to Disney World and not tell me you had sold my car to do it. Every time, I told myself this was the last time you were going to disappoint me. You would finally get your act together. But you never did. So it finally dawned on me that I was the problem. I believed in you too much."

A pair of elderly women huddled close together, eavesdropping.

Danny noticed and turned his back on them and said in a hushed tone, "Okay, so I made mistakes. But doesn't everybody deserve a second chance?"

"Yes. And a third. And sometimes even a fourth. I've given you countless chances, Danny. I lost track of how many, years ago. Now I don't want you creating this false impression in front of the kids that everything is hunky-dory between us because it's not. And they're old enough to handle it."

"Are we interrupting?" a woman purred behind Hayley.

Hayley turned and grimaced at the sight of Crystal Collier on the arm of Dr. Aaron, who looked supremely embarrassed to have happened upon Hayley arguing with her ex-husband.

Crystal, on the other hand, appeared utterly delighted.

"No, not at all," Hayley lied.

Aaron forced a smile.

His eyes full of sympathy.

"I just love this time of year. The crisp fall air. The leaves in full foliage," Crystal said. "Don't you agree?"

Danny nodded, suddenly distracted by something.

"How long are you planning to stay in town, Danny?" Aaron asked, trying to keep the conversation light and breezy.

Danny didn't answer.

He was focused on something.

Hayley tried following his gaze but she couldn't tell exactly what he was looking at so she tapped him on the shoulder. "Aaron asked you a question, Danny."

"What? Oh. I'm not sure yet," Danny said before hooking an arm around Hayley and pulling her away. "Come on, let's get a better view of the parade."

"But we have a perfect view right here," Hayley said before she was physically yanked away from Aaron and Crystal, who exchanged puzzled looks.

Hayley was still within earshot to hear Crystal say, "I think you dodged a bullet with that one."

She never heard Aaron's response.

And she wasn't sure she wanted to either.

"Danny, what's gotten into you? Slow down," Hayley said, resisting his grip.

But he was a man on a mission, and he tightened his hand that encircled her wrist, pulling her faster along as he led the way.

She looked around and was about to call for help when she spotted two men about ten feet behind them, seemingly in hot pursuit, and quickly closing in on them.

Two large muscular men, one bald and goateed and the other with a thick head of wavy black hair and a tan complexion, possibly Hispanic.

The same two men who were at the Criterion Theatre when Danny got spooked.

And possibly the same two men who were in that car parked outside Hayley's house presumably staking it out.

Suddenly, Danny broke into a run hauling Hayley along behind him.

"Danny, slow down, I'm wearing heels!"

They dashed into the middle of the parade jostling a boy in a giant blueberry costume and jumping over another little one dressed as Winnie the Pooh.

Hayley tripped over one little girl bedecked as one of the sisters from *Frozen* but she could never remember which one was Elsa and which one was Anna. As she tried to regain her balance, she twisted her ankle and felt a sharp pain.

She stumbled and Danny finally noticed and whipped his head around.

"Are you okay?"

"Yes. Now listen to me, Danny. I know you're being followed and I have an idea about how we can get rid of them. Just stick close to me and keep your mouth shut!" Hayley said, limping down the street.

Danny swiveled back around to see the two goons almost on top of them and then skedaddled after his ex-wife.

Hayley knew a police cruiser always brought up the rear of every parade in Bar Harbor. And she was guessing the two men tailing them would not be so anxious to get too close to the cops.

There were just a few scattered children, mostly third and fourth graders, left at the tail end of the parade when Hayley spotted the squad car rolling along slowly behind the last kid who appropriately enough was dressed as a cop complete with sunglasses and a badge while eating a doughnut.

Hayley practically hurled herself on top of the hood of the police cruiser. "Stop!"

Sergio was behind the wheel and hit the brakes.

"Come on! Get in!" Hayley screamed at Danny as she opened the back door and jumped in the car much to Sergio's surprise.

Danny followed, sliding in next to her and slamming the door shut.

The two musclemen stopped dead in their tracks and scowled as they watched Hayley and Danny drive past them.

Hayley watched as the two men immediately reversed course and disappeared back into the crowd of onlookers.

"Everything all right, Hayley?" Sergio asked, looking through the rearview mirror as Hayley massaged her bruised ankle.

"Who are they, Danny?" Hayley asked.

"Who?" Danny asked.

"Don't play games with me. I know those two men have been following you ever since you blew into town and you better tell me right now what they want with you."

Danny glanced at Hayley and then at Sergio, who was just as curious and anxious to hear how he was going to squirm out of this one.

Danny sighed. "Okay. Okay. Their names are Darryl Gillis and Logan Webster."

"And . . . ?" Hayley said, folding her arms.

"And they're a couple of guys I knew when I spent some time in Boston last month."

"What kind of guys?" Hayley asked.

"Guys. They're just a couple of guys," Danny barked.

"So if Sergio radios the station and has one of his

boys run those names through his computer, nothing out of the ordinary will turn up. Is that what you're saying?" Hayley asked.

Sergio nodded. "I can do that right now if you want me to."

"Yes. I think that would be very helpful, Sergio," Hayley said.

Danny paused and then said quietly, "Okay. You might find out that they're not exactly squeaky clean."

"And why is that?"

It was like pulling teeth getting Danny to admit the truth.

And it always had been.

"They work for a businessman in Boston who might be *slightly* Mafia-connected," Danny said, rubbing his eyes with the palms of his hand.

"Slightly? How is one *slightly* connected to the mafia?" Hayley bellowed. "And more importantly, how do *you* know them?"

"I got into a little trouble when I was there. I was trying to set up a new business venture. A real estate land deal. It was a sure thing . . ."

Hayley cut him off. "You can stop. I get it. You borrowed money from a loan shark and then skipped town instead of paying it back so Tony Soprano sent a couple of his goons to put a little pressure on you to come up with the money."

"Something like that, yeah," Danny said, eyes downcast, embarrassed.

"Stop the car, Sergio. I'm getting out," Hayley said.

"Now don't be mad . . ." Danny said, placing a hand on her shoulder, which she quickly shook off.

"I'm not mad, Danny. I'm tired. Tired of everything. Thanks for the lift, Sergio . . ."

"What about those two thugs, Hayley? You want me to send Donnie or Earl to keep an eye on your place in case they show up again?" Sergio asked as he pulled the cruiser over and put the gear in park.

"No, I'll call if I see anything out of the ordinary. Thanks, Sergio," she said before throwing open the door and jumping out.

She had momentarily forgotten about her ankle and another stinging pain shot through her leg as her heel hit the pavement.

Danny was out of the car in a flash and tried to steady her, but she didn't want his help. She threw out an arm, pushing him away, warning him to keep his distance.

She balanced herself.

Took a moment to regain her composure.

And then slowly turned to Danny.

"You came here knowing some bad guys were after you. You knew you were in a dangerous situation and yet you show up at my house and you worm your way back into our lives. What if those thugs decided to use your children to get you to pay up? Did you ever think about that? What if they kidnapped Gemma as she left the office or grabbed Dustin when he got off the school bus? Did you ever think about *that*?"

"No. I mean I'm fairly sure they wouldn't do that . . ."

"Fairly sure isn't good enough, Danny. Fairly sure

means it could have happened. When are you going to stop thinking about yourself? When are you ever going to take responsibility for your actions?"

"I'm trying to change . . ."

"You've been trying since the day I met you. It's never going to happen. I know it. The kids know it. The sooner you realize it the better off we'll all be."

She was done.

She whirled around to storm off but never even got to take a step. Because right in front of her were Gemma and Dustin, holding waffle cones, the pumpkin-flavored ice cream dripping down their hands as they watched the very public and very messy scene between their parents.

Hayley couldn't imagine feeling any worse.

Island Food & Spirits
by
Hayley Powell

My friend Mona popped by the house the other day for a cup of coffee. She timed her arrival because she knew I was making pumpkin muffins when she called earlier. Mona loved my muffins. She eagerly slathered one with a healthy scoop of cream cheese and gobbled it down. Mona had been eating these muffins ever since we were little girls and my mother was the one making them. Thankfully, Mom was willing to part with her secret recipe once I got married, and I've been happily baking them ever since. It was a much better wedding present than the toaster oven she bought for us that wasn't even on our registry but that's another story.

As much as I love pumpkin muffins, there was a time when I vowed never to make another batch as long as I lived.

It was some years back when Danny and I were still married and I spent two whole days whipping up batch after batch of muffins for the town bake sale held every year in the lobby of the town office. The money raised from the event was donated to the Bar Harbor Pet Pantry, which helped people feed their pets during the cold, harsh winter months.

Being an enthusiastic animal lover, I was more than happy to take part and sell my pumpkin muffins mostly because it was for such a worthy cause. However, I have to admit there was a small part of me that yearned to finally win Town Baker of the Year. The way it worked was whoever brought in the most money for their baked goods at the end of the two-hour sale had their portrait taken by a local photographer and their picture would hang for a whole year in the town office lobby.

I had been secretly dying to win this award for what seemed like forever, but for the last five years since entering the contest, I was constantly edged out by Karen Applebaum, a food writer for the *Bar Harbor Herald*. Karen fancied herself as Bar Harbor's go-to recipe expert, our local version of Julia Child, and despite my best efforts, Karen somehow always came out on top. This year, my ego refused to accept another defeat so I prepared like Rocky did for his big boxing match by baking and baking throughout the night until I had over two hundred muffins carefully placed in tins. I knew in my gut it was a winning recipe and I had the numbers. There was no way I could lose.

Stacking the tins in the back of my car, I drove over to the town office where everyone was already busy setting out their baked goods on assigned tables. I noticed Karen Applebaum was going to compete with her locally famous cherry pies. They all looked delicious but I was still feeling bullish about my muffins. Karen caught me staring. She gave my muffins a dismissive glance and looked away with a little condescending laugh.

She was trying to psych me out. Chip away at my confidence. But I was not going to allow that to happen. And as the townspeople began streaming in, many making a beeline for my muffins, I was confident I could pull out a win.

I put Mona in charge of grabbing more tins from the car as needed while I handled the cash transactions. With only a half hour left to go in the sale, I looked down to see just two muffins left. I was on a roll!

"Mona, I have two more tins in the back of my car! You better go get them!"

They were my reserve stash.

In case I needed them at the last minute to get me over the top.

Mona ran outside, but returned moments later, empty-handed.

Time was ticking.

"Where are the muffins?" I screeched.

"Your car's gone," Mona said.

"*What*?"

I noticed a last-minute surge at Karen Applebaum's table as a gathering crowd plucked the last of her cherry pies.

I needed those muffins stat!

I ran outside with Mona and sure enough my car was nowhere to be found. There was a red Volkswagen in the space where I had left it.

"Who would steal my muffins?"

I guess I should have been more concerned about the car but I was too consumed with my Town Baker of the Year title slipping through my fingers.

In the end, Karen Applebaum squeezed out a victory, but only by a few dollars. I vowed to take her down next year!

By the way, my car wasn't stolen. For once in his life, my husband, Danny, decided to surprise me and do an errand the first time I asked him instead of taking a day or two to get to it, which was his usual modus operandi. He had walked to the town office and taken the car across the street to the Shop 'n Save to do some grocery shopping before driving back across the street to pick me up and drive me home after the bake sale.

I should have been thrilled to discover the car was not stolen but I was inconsolable. When I got home I drowned my sorrows with a few Adult Pumpkin Milkshakes.

Yes, they're as delicious as they sound!

Mom's Pumpkin Muffins

<u>Ingredients</u>
¼ cup softened butter
½ cup sugar
¼ cup brown sugar
2 eggs, lightly beaten
2 tablespoons molasses
2 tablespoons grated orange peel
⅔ cup canned pumpkin
½ cup buttermilk
2 cups flour
1 teaspoon baking soda
½ teaspoon baking powder
1 teaspoon pumpkin pie spice
¼ teaspoon salt

Streusel Topping

Ingredients

⅓ cup flour

3 tablespoons brown sugar

2 tablespoons cold butter

In a large mixing bowl cream together your butter and sugars until fluffy. Beat in the pumpkin, buttermilk, eggs, molasses and orange zest.

In a separate bowl combine the flour, baking soda, baking powder, pumpkin pie spice, and salt. Slowly add to the pumpkin mixture just until blended.

Fill your paper-lined or greased muffin tin ⅔ full.

To Prepare the Topping

In a bowl combine your flour and sugar. Add your cold butter and cut it in until the mixture is crumbly. Sprinkle the mixture over the tops of your muffins.

Bake in a preheated 375-degree oven for 20 to 25 minutes or until a toothpick comes out clean. Remove from oven and cool for about five minutes, then remove them from the pan and cool on wire rack.

* * *

Adult Pumpkin Milkshakes

<u>Ingredients</u>
2 cups of your favorite vanilla ice
    cream
½ can pumpkin puree
3 ounces of your favorite bourbon
⅓ cup half-and-half
2 tablespoons maple syrup
½ teaspoon pumpkin pie spice

Place all your ingredients in a blender and blend well, then pour into frosty glasses and indulge yourself with this soothing treat with a kick!

Chapter 26

"I'm going to cut right to the chase, Hayley," Crystal Collier said, leaning back in her office chair and crossing her shapely legs. "I need to know if you still harbor feelings for Aaron."

Hayley certainly appreciated her directness.

She was amazed at the number of warnings to stay away from men she had received recently.

First Becky.

Now Crystal.

Although this was not what she was expecting when Crystal called her at the office and told her she would like to see her if she could manage to swing by her office during her lunch hour.

Crystal offered to have some curried chicken salad and a bottle of Perrier waiting for her if she agreed. Hayley told herself it wasn't the prospect of a free lunch that convinced her to accept Crystal's invitation.

Because it wasn't.

Although she loved curried chicken.

And her mouth was watering just thinking about it after she hung up the phone with Crystal.

So it was probably time to admit she was lying to herself.

Still, she was curious at to why it was so important Crystal speak with her.

And now she knew.

Crystal was threatened by her past relationship with Aaron.

Just like Becky was threatened by her past relationship with Danny.

She sincerely hoped there wasn't anyone else in town threatened by her.

Hayley intended to be completely honest with Crystal and wanted her to be reassured that she had completely moved on from Aaron.

But Crystal was so dismissive and condescending at the pet costume contest and so overtly thrilled to witness marital discord, or rather, ex-marital discord between her and Danny at the Halloween parade, she had half a mind to put on a show and work up some fake tears and tell Crystal she had never stopped loving Aaron.

Hayley picked up her plastic fork and stabbed a piece of chicken out of the plastic container and popped it in her mouth. "Why? Did Aaron say something?"

"Oh no. Aaron has made his feelings for me crystal clear. Pardon the pun," Crystal said, smiling, pleased with her own clever little joke.

It wasn't *that* clever.

But Hayley kept her opinion to herself.

"You haven't dated anyone that I know of since you and Aaron ended things, and I'm sure your

ex-husband showing up again has hindered any
chance of meeting someone new, and so I just need
to know where I stand when it comes to your feelings about Aaron," Crystal said, adopting a loose and
friendly tone, but staring at Hayley's ratty drab-
brown sweater, her eyes dripping with judgment and
disapproval.

Crystal could certainly afford to look down on
Hayley's bargain-basement sweater because she was
wearing a sleek BOSS Kadine jacket over a stylish
Hildine dress from Saks Fifth Avenue that had probably set her back at least a grand.

Hayley knew this because she subscribed to every
fashion catalog and browsed through them reli-
giously even though she knew she could barely
afford to buy a wallet to house her maxed-out credit
cards.

"Why is this so important for you to know?"
Hayley asked, suddenly self-conscious and folding
her arms in a failed attempt to hide her sweater.

"I just want some peace of mind that we won't en-
counter any obstacles when we move on to the next
level," Crystal said as she shuffled some paperwork
on her desk as if she were multitasking while having
this supposedly serious conversation with Hayley.

As if Hayley wasn't worthy of her undivided attention.

"You mean *marriage*?" Hayley gasped before
quickly recovering and adding, "That's wonderful.
Congratulations."

"Don't put words in my mouth," Crystal said although she was obviously thrilled Hayley had
jumped to that conclusion. "I just want everything

out in the open before we move forward on any future plans together."

She was being very careful and lawyerly in her responses, which made Hayley annoyed and more than a little bit nervous.

Lawyers always made her uncomfortable.

And at this point she just wanted to finish her curried chicken salad and get the hell out of there.

Enough games.

It was time to put Crystal's mind at ease.

"Let me assure you, Crystal. I have no plans to rekindle the flame with Aaron. It's over. It has been for a long time. And I'm happy where I am now. And I'm happy he's found someone."

Crystal studied Hayley's face like a map, searching for any sign she was not being completely honest and forthright. And then, finally satisfied, she broke out into a wide albeit insincere smile. "Thank you. That's all I wanted to hear."

Hayley felt relieved Crystal believed her.

Unlike Becky who wasn't so easy to convince regarding Danny.

Hayley noticed a stack of papers sitting on the edge of Crystal's large, expensive oak desk.

Crystal saw her glancing at it.

"It's a new horror novel from an author I represent," Crystal offered.

"Norman Cross?"

"I'm afraid that's confidential because the author is a client."

"I understand."

Hayley stole a look at the title.

The Devil's Honeymoon.

The space underneath the title where the writer's name was usually listed was blank.

Crystal's phone buzzed and she pressed a button. "Yes, Yvette?"

A young woman's disembodied voice said, "The Sanborn papers are here for you to countersign. Shall I bring them in?"

"No, I'll come out," Crystal said, standing up and walking around her desk. "Enjoy your lunch, Hayley. I'll be right back."

She headed out and shut the door behind her.

Hayley reached for the plastic container of curried chicken when she suddenly stopped.

Something was gnawing at her.

It was the title of the manuscript.

The Devil's Honeymoon.

She had heard it before.

Of course!

It was the same title as Spanky McFarland's book.

Hayley stood up, turned to make sure Crystal hadn't walked back in her office, and quickly began leafing through the pages.

Kurt and Lila.

The young newlyweds.

Arriving in a small coastal tourist town much like Bar Harbor.

Hayley flipped through some more pages.

The townspeople were unfriendly and remote.

Acting strange.

The young couple were spooked and ready to blow town.

But a series of unfortunate events prevented them from leaving.

Hayley fanned the pages until she reached the last third of the book.

She scanned the last few chapters.

The whole town's population were actually disciples of the devil.

This manuscript wasn't just similar to Spanky's book.

It *was* Spanky's book!

And Hayley had a sickening feeling that the author Crystal Collier was representing was not her son Dustin's fifteen-year-old best friend.

Chapter 27

"Your father could have forged that paper," Hayley said as she set three rows of corn taco shells down on a baking pan and slid them in the oven in her kitchen.

"Sergio doesn't think so. The signature matches a few other signed documents Otis had in a file drawer," Gemma said, shredding lettuce and chopping tomatoes on a cutting board.

Hayley was deeply skeptical about what the police found after meticulously going through all of the late Otis Pearson's belongings recovered at his cabin in the hopes of finding a reason someone would want him dead.

What turned up was a signed will from Otis, nothing official or notarized, but stating it was his wish that Danny be bequeathed the remaining amount of his life savings in the event of his death.

"So does this mean Sergio's going to drop the theft charge?" Hayley asked.

"It looks that way. Although he was still mad at Dad for jumping the gun and taking the money before the investigation was completed and the will was recovered," Gemma said, scraping the lettuce and tomatoes off the cutting board and onto the plate.

Hayley stirred a bubbling skillet of seasoned taco meat with a wooden spoon. "Well, he's still in the doghouse. He came here with the Boston Mafia on his tail and put us all in danger."

"He didn't know they were chasing him until after he got here. And Dad told me he used most of his inheritance from Otis to pay off his debt so those two guys who were following him around have already gone back to Boston. Everything's fine now," Gemma said, sliding a block of cheddar cheese up and down a steel shredder. "I just hate thinking of him staying all alone in that fleabag motel."

Hayley tasted a small piece of sizzling taco meat to test the seasoning.

She added some more chili pepper. "If I let him come stay here again, you and Dustin need to know . . ."

"It's only temporary. You're never getting back together. We get it, Mom. Seriously. But we hardly ever see him and he's only going to be in town a few more days and it would be nice having him around," Gemma said.

"Let me think about," Hayley said, sighing. "Now go call your brother for supper."

Gemma smiled, knowing she had won the argument and her mother would cave. She bounced out of the kitchen and called up the stairs. "Tacos are ready!"

Dustin bounded down the stairs with Spanky right behind him.

When Hayley arrived home from work, she hadn't expected to see Spanky hanging out in Dustin's room discussing their film adaptation of his horror novel. And Dustin was surprised his mother so readily invited Spanky to stay for supper, unaware she had an ulterior motive.

The boys took their places at the dining room table as Gemma set out the bowl of taco meat, plate of warm shells, and all the fixings.

Hayley retrieved the homemade guacamole she had prepared earlier from the fridge and then joined the kids at the table as they began making their tacos.

"So how's the book coming along, Spanky?" Hayley casually asked as she watched him stuffing his shell with meat and vegetables.

Spanky shrugged. "Good."

"Tell us more. It's all very exciting," Hayley said. "Have you heard from Mr. Cross yet?"

Spanky shrugged. "No."

"He's not supposed to talk about it," Dustin said, shutting his mother down.

"Why not?"

Spanky took a big bite out of his taco and chewed.

"Who told you not to talk about it?" Hayley asked.

"My mother always yells at me for talking with my mouth full," Spanky said, bits of taco shell and strands of cheese falling out of his mouth.

"Well, I'll wait," Hayley said, determined to find out more.

They all waited as Spanky chewed and chewed and chewed before finally swallowing the food in his mouth in one big gulp.

He went to take another bite of the taco in his hand while the sauce dripped down his hand and onto the table. Hayley reached out and grabbed his wrist before the messy taco could reach his mouth. "Who told you not to talk about it, Spanky?"

"Shane."

And then he crunched down and bit off another hunk.

"Mr. Cross's writing assistant?"

Spanky nodded.

Crunch, crunch, crunch.

After another big swallow, Spanky wiped his mouth with a napkin and said, "He said it was probably best, at least until Mr. Cross has had a chance to read my book."

"What else did Shane tell you?" Hayley asked.

But she was too late.

Spanky shoved the remaining taco deep inside his mouth.

Crunch, crunch, crunch.

Hayley waited patiently.

Even Gemma and Dustin were now curious and leaning forward, impatiently waiting for Spanky to swallow.

Spanky smiled at them as he continued chewing.

Taking his time.

Savoring the spicy taco meat.

Finally, after what felt like an eternity, Spanky swallowed and everyone at the table held their breath in anticipation.

"Nothing."

"Really? That's it? That's all we get?" Gemma said, throwing her napkin down on the table.

"Shane's really nice. I think he wants to be a writer too. That's why he's trying to help me out. We have a lot in common."

Spanky reached for another taco shell and began filling it up.

Hayley wasn't ready to tell the poor boy she had seen his original manuscript lying on top of Crystal Collier's desk.

No, she had to find out more about this Shane Hardy first.

for an interview.

"I remember Shane had a very strong taste for
older women. He used to hit on all his female profes-
sors. Including me," Judith Ann Moore said as she
walked with Hayley across the campus of the College of the Atlantic, located just outside of town
where Professor Moore had an office. "He was also
a very driven young man, dare I say ruthless, willing
to do anything to become a published author,"

It was a brisk afternoon, leaves blowing all around
from a gusty wind, and Judith Ann buttoned up her
fleece coat to keep warm. She was an attractive
woman in her early seventies, with a heart-shaped
face and infectious smile. She had to keep tucking
her long dyed-blond hair behind her ears to keep it
from blowing around and covering her eyes.

That morning Hayley had asked Sal during the
staff meeting if he had heard of Shane Hardy. Sal
knew the name but didn't know much about him. But
it was Bruce who recalled the young man applying
for an internship position at the *Island Times* a few

years back, when he was still in college, to shadow a reporter and learn more about the day-to-day workings of newspaper journalism.

After Sal adjourned the meeting, Hayley searched the files on her computer and very quickly found Shane's application. His résumé lacked experience, which wasn't surprising for his young age, and his essay on why he wanted to work at the paper was brief and uninspired, but he still had been brought in for an interview.

Only after meeting with Sal here at the office was he rejected for the position.

Sal had no recollection of meeting with him, nor what they talked about, or why he wasn't hired. Bruce remembered running into Shane the day he came in to meet with Sal, and did recall thinking at the time that he was a rather "odd bird," but beyond that, he made very little impression on anyone.

Hayley figured she must have been running an errand or out that day dealing with a "kid emergency" because she had no memory of him whatsoever.

One detail on his application did stand out.

He purported to have studied with Judith Ann Moore, a writing professor at the local college.

Judith Ann and Hayley's mother, Sheila, had grown up together. They lived next door to each other when they were little girls until the famous 1947 Bar Harbor fire swept through town ravaging homes and businesses not to mention acres of forests in Acadia National Park.

Hayley's grandparents' house on Greeley Avenue where her mother lived had been hosed down and spared but Judith Ann's house right next door was decimated. Her family had to move in with relatives until they could rebuild. Sheila and Judith Ann remained friends throughout the years, the devastating loss from the tragedy bonding them even more, and they were still tight to this day. Once a year when her classes were not in session, Judith Ann would book a cheap flight down to Florida and spend quality time with her childhood best friend.

So it was easy for Hayley to pick up the phone and call Judith Ann, and see if she would mind Hayley swinging by the college that afternoon to ask her a few questions about a former student.

"'Ruthless' is a pretty strong word," Hayley said, her lips quivering from the chilly late fall air. "How ruthless?"

Judith Ann took a deep breath. "I had a student, Connor Newman, who was very talented and well respected by his peers for his exceptional writing ability. He came to me and accused Shane of plagiarizing one of his short stories. He had asked Shane to read it and give him some notes, and Shane had come back with several pages of thoughts and so Connor decided to write a new draft. But before he was able to finish the revisions, his original story was published in the student literary journal under Shane's name. I brought Shane in and asked him about it and he adamantly denied any wrongdoing and said if anyone had stolen the story it was Connor. I couldn't prove that Shane had plagiarized the story because according to Connor he never showed anyone else the piece before Shane. So it was Connor's word against Shane's."

"But your instinct told you Shane was the guilty party," Hayley said.

Judith Ann nodded. "I was certain. But there wasn't anything I could do about it."

"And that was the end of it," Hayley said.

"Not quite," Judith Ann said, trying one more time to tuck her long hair behind her ear to keep it out of her face as the winds whipped up all around them. "Connor wouldn't let it go. He tried to involve the student peer committee, the college president, the board of trustees. The more actions he took the angrier he made Shane and there was a rumor . . ."

"What rumor?"

Judith Ann hesitated.

"What rumor, Judith Ann?"

"Let me be clear, Hayley, the rumor was never substantiated. It was just talk."

"I understand. Please tell me."

Judith Ann took another deep breath. "I've never spoken about this to anyone because it's in the past and nothing was ever proven. But just as Connor seemed to be making progress with the administration and there was actually talk of a formal investigation . . ."

"Go on . . ." Hayley said, unable to stand the suspense much longer.

"Connor dropped out. He had his parents pick him up and take him home to Connecticut."

"Why? What happened?"

"Nobody knows. But there was a story going around campus that Connor was at a party and Shane brought him a cocktail made with lemonade as sort of a peace offering. But very quickly Connor got sick and had to be rushed to the hospital. He almost died. The doctors assumed he had drunk too much and was suffering from alcohol poisoning. They pumped his stomach and mercifully he pulled through. But there were some very scary moments until they were able to stabilize him."

"Did Connor have a lot to drink before running into Shane?"

"No. He claimed he had just arrived at the party and was stone-cold sober. Alcohol poisoning didn't make any sense."

"So what caused him to get sick?"

"Apparently there was a girl at the party who saw Shane spiking the lemonade with some kind of poison . . ."

"He was trying to *kill* Connor?"

"Or scare him so bad that he would stop trying to come after him."

"I guess it worked," Hayley said, stunned. "Did the police talk to the girl who witnessed Shane spiking the lemonade?"

Judith Ann shook her head. "No. Like I said, it was just a story. And the girl didn't want to come forward and get involved. Connor left town shortly after that without taking any tests to prove it was something else besides too much alcohol in his system. So with no witness or any physical evidence, the whole matter was dropped. And frankly, the administration was relieved. What would it look like if one of their students was caught trying to poison a classmate?"

"And so Shane continued his studies as if nothing had happened?"

"Yes. And that story he purportedly stole won a national student literary award. He even got a small cash prize."

Hayley couldn't believe it.

Just like Judith Ann's instinct, Hayley's gut was telling her the rumor was true.

And history was about to repeat itself.

She was certain Shane Hardy had no intention of ever showing Spanky's horror novel to Norman Cross.

He was going to steal it and claim it as his own.

Island Food & Spirits
by
Hayley Powell

My ex-husband, Danny, who has been visiting the island recently, took my two kids to the Cross House of Horrors last night, and I decided it was a good time to face my own house of horrors when I noticed a dust bunny the size of a small rodent floating across my living room floor. The house was in dire need of a thorough cleaning. So after whipping up a batch of my yummy Pumpkin Chocolate Chip Cookies for when my kids returned home later that evening, I decided to get to it.

I had only done a quick dusting and sweeping of the living room, when I thought I heard a Pumpkin Mojito calling my name. I thought for a second I should wait to reward myself until I at least finished cleaning the downstairs, but true to form, I ignored that thought and found myself rummaging through the cupboards for a bottle of rum.

I served Pumpkin Mojitos to Danny on the first Halloween after we got married and it quickly became an annual tradition. A lot of people wondered why Danny chose me to marry when he had his pick of any girl in town, given his good looks and charming ways. Danny loved flirting with his admirers and there was no denying he had a roving eye for the pretty ladies. I begrudgingly accepted this basic fact until one night after we returned home from a cocktail party where I might have been slightly over served with alcohol. I was steaming over his ignoring me at the party while talking up a set of pretty blonde triplets. I warned him that if he didn't start paying more attention to me he might be better off making other living arrangements in the near future!

Apparently he took my threat seriously because the next thing I knew we were in a cabin on Moosehead Lake in Greenville, Maine, ice fishing for a week. Just the two of us. Not exactly the romantic getaway to Paris or Belize I would have preferred, but I was going to take what I could get!

Danny wasn't exactly one to plan ahead. He mistakenly thought that eating our ice fishing catch of the day would be a romantic adventure, two people off the grid, living off the land, in love in the wild. Well, after almost three days eating fish for breakfast, lunch, and dinner, with a side of peanut butter on bread, we had both had enough! So he decided to take the car and drive to a general store in town and stock up on some much needed meats, vegetables, potatoes, and junk food! I opted to remain cozy by the roaring fire happily reading my new Danielle Steel novel.

Well, I was so engrossed in my book that I didn't realize how long he had been gone until my stomach began to rumble and I glanced up at the clock and was surprised to see it was already six PM! Danny had been gone for three hours!

That's when I remembered the general store was also attached to the local bar and restaurant. Groceries, my butt! That cad probably popped into the local watering hole and was now drinking a few beers and chatting up some dewey-eyed, adoring bimbo.

I got so riled up I grabbed my heavy coat, hat, and gloves and ran outside. Of course there was no car. Danny had taken it into town. And there was no way in hell I was going to walk the three long miles in freezing bear country! I was stuck here while Danny was enjoying himself and doing God only knew what! Suddenly I noticed to my left the snowmobile that came with the cabin for our personal use. I had been riding them since I was a kid, and so I jumped on it, cranked the key, and took off flying down the plowed road ready for a showdown with that no-good husband of mine!

The ride was bitterly cold and I couldn't feel my face as wet slush kicked up by the snowmobile covered me from head to toe. I kept my eyes peeled for a rogue moose or unsuspecting deer that might inadvertently step in front of me. Luckily I made it into town safely. Bundled up and covered in snowy slush, I must have looked like a wild, crazed mountain man as I stomped into the general store/bar/restaurant. Several patrons turned and stared at me, and I think I may have growled at them to keep their distance as I scanned the room.

And then I spotted him. His back was to me. He was in a booth with a toothy redhead in a tight-fitting red wool sweater. Danny's head was bobbing up and down seeming to hang on every word that poured out of her bright red painted lips. Dolly Parton's "Jolene" was playing on the jukebox. And Dolly's words pierced through me as she sang her lyrics about not taking her man just because you can.

I love Dolly.

I stormed across the bar, grabbed a full pitcher of beer off a table much to the surprise of the two men who were just about to pour themselves a glass, marched straight over to my husband, and dumped the entire pitcher of cold beer down over his head while yelling, "I've caught you red-handed, you lying, good-for-nothing cheat!"

And then I turned to that sneaky harlot sitting across from him. "In case you didn't know, Jolene, he's married!"

The room fell silent.

The girl looked at me dumbfounded. "My name is Sally Ann."

I didn't miss a beat.

"In case you didn't know, Sally Ann, he's married!"

And then I set the pitcher down on the table and without saying another word, I turned on my heels and walked with what dignity I could muster toward the exit back into the store. Halfway there I froze in my tracks. There in front of me was Danny Powell standing in the doorway holding a bag of groceries in one arm and a dozen red roses in the other (the general store also boasted a florist shop). His mouth was agape and his eyes were wide open after witnessing his wife's dramatic scene.

I just looked up and whispered, "Oh Lord, please just take me now."

Luckily Danny is also a smooth talker and his charm works on men as well as women. He's a likable guy. And after some fast talking and a promise to pay for the couple's bar bill and dinner, we were finally on our way back to the cabin, leaving the snowmobile to be picked up the next day when it was light out.

Danny quietly told me on the car ride home that he got a flat tire on the way to the store. He didn't have a replacement tire so he hitched a ride into town from some high school kids passing by on the main road, had our tire repaired, and then hitched another ride with a snowplow driver back to change out the flat before driving back into town for the groceries. The timeline added up to three hours. Oops.

Let's just say after that, I was the one in the doghouse! But true to Danny's nature, after six months of good behavior, I caught Danny flirting with Bethany, the cute cashier at the Shop 'n Save, and he was back in the doghouse once again, right where he belonged!

* * *

Hayley's Pumpkin Chocolate Chip Cookies

<u>Ingredients</u>
1 stick of butter melted (½ cup)
¼ cup brown sugar
½ cup granulated sugar
1 teaspoon vanilla
6 tablespoons pumpkin puree
1½ cups flour
¼ teaspoon salt
¼ teaspoon baking powder
½ teaspoon cinnamon
¼ teaspoon nutmeg
¼ teaspoon ground cloves
½ cup chocolate chips

In a bowl mix your melted butter, brown sugar, and granulated sugar together. Whisk in the vanilla and pumpkin puree.

In a large bowl mix together your flour, salt, baking soda, baking powder, cinnamon, nutmeg, and cloves. Pour your wet ingredients into your dry and mix together. This dough will be soft. Mix in your chocolate chips and cover and chill in the fridge for at least 30 minutes or up to 3 days.

Line your baking sheets with parchment paper and remove dough from fridge. Take rounded tablespoons full of dough, make balls, and place on cookie sheets. Lightly flatten with

your hand. Bake in a preheated oven
for 10 minutes then remove from oven.
Cool slightly and then place on wire
rack to finish cooling.

Pumpkin Mojito

<u>Ingredients</u>
8 mint leaves
1 tablespoon brown sugar
1½ ounces rum
1 tablespoon pumpkin puree
Juice of half a lime
2 ounces club soda

Add your mint leaves and brown
sugar to the bottom of a cocktail shaker
and muddle together.
Add your rum, pumpkin puree, and
lime, and shake until very well mixed.
Strain into a glass and top with club
soda.

Chapter 29

Hayley's head was spinning as she drove back to the *Island Times* office after leaving the College of the Atlantic. She kept one eye on the road as she scrolled through her list of contacts on her phone to find Carla McFarland.

With her thumb, she hit Carla's number and then slammed the phone to her ear as she impatiently waited for her to answer the call.

After four interminable rings, she heard Carla say, "McFarland residence. This is Carla."

"Carla, it's Hayley Powell."

"Oh, hello, Hayley. Hey, have you given any thought as to what you're baking for the upcoming PTA—"

"Not now, Carla! This is very important. Is Spanky at home with you right now?"

"Well, gosh, I don't know. I just walked through the door and I'm putting away groceries. Why? Is anything the matter?"

"Would you check his room, please?"

There was a pause as Carla considered Hayley's panicky tone.

"Hayley, you're making me nervous . . ."

"Please, Carla, just check to see if Spanky is home."

"Hold on."

Carla put down the phone.

Hayley suddenly had to jerk the wheel and swerve her car over the yellow line to avoid a wide-eyed squirrel dashing from one side of the road to the other. The little creature made it within inches of his life, much to Hayley's relief. She didn't need roadkill splattered all over the bottom of her new set of Cooper tires.

After about a minute, Carla was back on the phone. "No, he's not. What's going on, Hayley? What's happened?"

Hayley suddenly realized the last thing she should do at the moment was to scare Carla unnecessarily. After all, she had no proof Spanky was in some kind of real danger or that Shane Hardy was any kind of imminent threat. She only knew that someone was passing off Spanky's story as his or her own, and that according to his former teacher Judith Ann, the most likely suspect was Shane Hardy.

But the attempted-murder-of-a-rival-student story she had heard from Judith Ann was at this point just that.

A story.

"It's nothing, Carla. Did Spanky happen to leave you a note or a phone message letting you know where he is?"

"No. The only message on the machine was from that young man who works for Norman Cross. Shane something. He just said for Spanky to call him back as soon as possible."

Hayley's heart leapt into her throat.

But she tried to remain calm for Carla's sake.

She could be wrong about this whole thing.

"Well, when he comes home would you please give me a call and let me know?"

"You've got me twisted up in knots, Hayley. What's this all about?"

"I'm just looking for Dustin, that's all. And we both know where you find Spanky you will usually find Dustin."

"Well, that's for sure," Carla said, laughing, a hint of relief in her voice.

Hayley hung up just as she squealed to a stop in front of the office of the *Island Times*, where the sun had already set and darkness was slowly enveloping the town. She jumped out of her Kia and raced up the sidewalk.

The door to the office was locked.

She fished through her ring of keys, unlocked the door, and hurried inside.

All the lights were off.

It was past five and the whole staff had already gone home.

Hayley clicked on her recent calls and speed-dialed Bruce Linney's number.

She tapped her foot, impatiently waiting for him to answer.

"This is Bruce Linney, I'm unable to take your call right now . . ."

"Damn it, Bruce! Why don't you ever pick up?"

". . . so leave a message and I will return your call just as soon as I can."

Beep.

"Bruce, it's Hayley. It's urgent I talk to you. I need your help. Call me the second you get this message."

She ended the call.

She knew she couldn't wait until she heard back from Bruce.

There was a chance Spanky was already on his way to Norman Cross's mansion to meet Shane Hardy, or God forbid he was already there, and what if Shane at this very moment was implementing his evil plan to bump off the poor unsuspecting boy, thus disposing of any evidence that *The Devil's Honeymoon* was written by anyone but him?

But she couldn't go over there alone.

It was too dangerous.

She was counting on Bruce to be her bodyguard and protector.

But Bruce Linney was AWOL.

She had to call somebody.

And then *his* name popped into her head.

He was the only one she could think of at the moment.

She hated calling him.

But time was of the essence.

Hayley bolted out of the *Island Times* office back to her car, her phone clamped to her ear.

After one ring, he picked up.

"Hello?"

"Danny, it's me."

"Oh hey, babe, I was just thinking of you as I'm lying on top of this ratty, bug-infested bed in this nearly condemned tenement they call a motel . . ."

"Danny, I don't have time for this. I need your

help. Be out front in five minutes. I'm driving by to pick you up."

As she screeched around the corner, Danny was standing there waiting with a big grin on his face.

He was relishing the fact he had actually heard Hayley say the words "*I need your help.*"

Hayley barely rolled the car to a stop and he had to jog a little bit after opening the passenger side door just to keep up so he could jump inside before she roared away.

After he strapped himself in with the seatbelt, Hayley quickly brought him up to speed and his smile slowly faded at the seriousness of the situation.

When they pulled up in front of Norman Cross's home, it was already pitch-black outside. The one streetlight on the corner was busted so the only source of light was coming from inside the mansion. A few dim lamps downstairs and five flickering candles in the upstairs windowsills.

Hayley and Danny pushed their way through the rusty, squeaky wrought-iron gate and up the dirt path to the main house, where they ascended the creaky porch steps before reaching the front door.

Hayley rang the bell.

They waited about a minute and then Danny banged his fist on the door several times.

After another few seconds the door slowly opened and Shane Hardy was there to greet them with a pleasant yet crooked smile. "May I help you?"

"We're looking for Spanky," Hayley said.

"I'm sorry, who?" Shane asked, not quite placing the name.

Or pretending not to place the name.

"Spanky McFarland," Danny said. "We have reason to believe he's here."

"I can assure you he's not," Shane said emphatically. "Who is he again?"

"I'm sure you remember him. You promised to show his manuscript to Mr. Cross just as soon as he was feeling better," Hayley said.

Shane reacted as if a light bulb had just gone off inside his head. "Oh, yes. Spanky. Now I remember him. He was a big fan of Mr. Cross. He kept showing up on the doorstep asking to meet him. It was cute at first but he very quickly became a nuisance so I had to shoo him away."

"What about the manuscript?" Hayley asked, eyeing him suspiciously.

"I promise you I have no idea what you're talking about," Shane said, recoiling like a copperhead snake, his long hair falling in front of his face.

"I don't believe you," Hayley said.

"Fortunately it makes no difference whether you believe me or not," Shane said, moving to close the door.

Danny stopped it with his boot.

"Spanky! Are you in there?" Hayley yelled.

"I told you he's not here!" Shane growled.

Danny shoved the door open, surprising Shane who stumbled back. "I'm sure you don't mind if we take a look-see for ourselves just to make sure."

Hayley was impressed by Danny's bravado and followed him inside.

They looked around but the living room and parlor were empty.

It was deathly quiet.

The only sound in the room was from a crackling fire in the fireplace.

"I could call the police and have you removed, but my mother taught me the proper etiquette of being a good host. So I'm going to ignore the fact that you just pushed your way in here uninvited and I'm going to treat you as my guests," Shane said.

"You mean Mr. Cross's guests. This is Mr. Cross's home," Hayley said.

"Yes, of course," Shane said through gritted teeth. "Now, let's all try to calm down. Why don't you have a seat in the parlor and perhaps I can help you find this boy Spanky? How does that sound? Can I offer you a drink? Some of my freshly squeezed lemonade?"

A shiver shot up Hayley's spine.

"No! No lemonade!" she blurted out.

Shane nodded and turned to Danny. "What about you, sir? It's my special recipe."

"Sure. Why not? I'll try some."

Hayley's heart nearly stopped beating.

Chapter 30

"Make yourselves comfortable in the parlor and I'll be right back," Shane said, turning and retreating into the kitchen to fetch his likely poisonous concoction.

Hayley grabbed Danny by the arm. "I don't have time to explain but whatever you do, do *not* drink that lemonade."

"But I'm thirsty," Danny whined.

"For once in your life, just listen to what I'm saying, okay, Danny? Do not drink the lemonade. I don't want the kids losing their father while they're still young!"

Danny's eyes widened at her last comment and he nodded his head.

Hayley's phone buzzed and she scooped it out of her coat pocket.

There was a text from Carla McFarland.

Spanky and Dustin just got here. They were at Toby Alley's house playing video games after school and lost track of time. I told Dustin to go directly home because you were looking for him.

Hayley heaved a huge sigh of relief.

"Everything good?" Danny asked.

"Yes. He's home safe."

"Good. Then we can get the hell out of here."

Shane entered with a pitcher of lemonade and two glasses. He winked at Hayley. "I brought an extra glass in case you change your mind."

"We're going to have to take a rain check," Danny said.

"Did you find your lost boy?" Shane asked, feigning interest.

"Yes. He's home with his mother," Hayley said.

"See? All that worrying for nothing," Shane said, pouring lemonade into one of the glasses, filling it all the way up to the rim. "Are you sure you don't want some?"

"Yeah, I'm sure," Danny said, furtively glancing at Hayley.

She kept her eyes fixed on Shane. "So tell me about your new book, Shane."

"What new book?" he asked, a puzzled look on his face.

"*The Devil's Honeymoon*," Hayley said, hitting every word.

There was a flicker of concern on his face.

For a brief second.

Then he got it hastily under control and kept that same bland, insincere, nonthreatening crooked smile on his face.

But he was at a loss for words.

He obviously hadn't expected to hear that title roll off someone else's lips.

The Devil's Honeymoon.

He was fighting to remain unruffled.

But it was a challenge.

Hayley could tell on the inside he was freaking out.

"I'm not sure what you're talking about," Shane said, standing motionless after setting the pitcher of lemonade down on the tray.

"I saw the manuscript in your lawyer's office," Hayley said. "Crystal Collier is representing you, isn't that right? She's acting as your literary agent and contract lawyer. At least that's what she told me."

She hadn't told her the client was Shane.

But he didn't have to know that.

"I'm sure she didn't . . . ." Shane said, his voice cracking.

"She most certainly did. Shane Hardy. The hot new author who was going to be the next Norman Cross," Hayley said.

Shane just kept shaking his head. "No . . . No . . . she didn't . . ."

"The funny thing is I had seen that title before. *The Devil's Honeymoon.* On the cover of the manuscript Spanky McFarland brought over to my house just over a week ago."

"You can't copyright a title. Lots of books have the same title," Shane said weakly.

"You're right," Hayley said. "But you see, when Crystal left her office for a few minutes I took a moment to skim your book. Imagine my surprise when I read a few pages only to discover it was the exact same story with the exact same characters, all with the same names, as Spanky's book."

"The boy was here in this house. He could have gotten his hands on *my* manuscript and made a copy for himself to claim as his own," Shane spit out.

"Yes, but your mistake was thinking that Spanky

was a loner, a misfit, with no friends. But he and my son are best buddies, and my son has been a witness to Spanky's creative process every step of the way, for months, long before you even thought to pretend you were working on your own book."

"But I made him promise he hadn't—" Shane stopped himself.

"Shown anyone else the book? You can't blame the boy for lying. I think I'd say just about anything if it meant getting my hero to read my work."

"This is all just a huge misunderstanding . . ." Shane sputtered.

"Does Mr. Cross know what you've been up to?" Hayley asked.

"Hey, I have an idea. Why don't we go ask him?" Danny said, stepping toward the staircase.

Shane snapped out of his shock to throw his body in front of the steps, blocking Danny's path.

"I told you he's not feeling well. He's resting right now and cannot accept visitors!" Shane cried.

But Danny was bigger and bulkier and Shane was no match for him. Danny flung him to the side like a straw-filled scarecrow and mounted the stairs.

Shane watched helplessly as Hayley pushed past him and followed Danny up to the master suite.

Danny was already inside the bedroom when Hayley caught up with him.

He was standing in the middle of the room just staring at the bed.

Hayley came up on his left and stopped next to him.

The room was empty.

The bed was made.

There was no sign of Norman Cross.

They heard Shane huffing and puffing behind them as he entered the room.

Danny whirled around and barked, "Where is he? You said he was resting. What have you done with him?"

Hayley gasped at the sight of Shane Hardy, standing in the doorway, gripping a semiauto rimfire pistol in his right hand.

Chapter 31

Hayley and Danny both stiffened as they slowly raised their hands in the air.

Shane pointed the gun at them.

His hand was shaking.

He was agitated and panicked. "Now just stand there quietly for a minute and let me think."

His eyes darted back and forth.

Danny shifted a little to his right and the sudden move startled Shane, who thrust the gun out, his finger waffling on the trigger.

"I said don't move!"

Danny realized Shane was on the verge of hysteria and just might accidentally shoot without even meaning to, so he stood frozen in place alongside Hayley.

"Shane . . ." Hayley said softly and gently.

Shane pointed the gun at Hayley. "Shush! Please! I told you I'm trying to think!"

Hayley nodded and glanced over at Danny, who kept his eyes glued on the gun.

Finally, Shane made a decision.

With his free hand, he reached into his back pocket and whipped out his cell phone. He pressed a button and clamped the phone to his ear, waiting for someone to answer.

The wait seemed endless.

But it only lasted a few seconds.

Shane stood upright as someone picked up the call. He lowered the gun slightly but it was still pointed in Hayley and Danny's direction and Shane's finger still rested loosely on the trigger. "It's me. I've got a big problem. It's that nosy newspaper reporter Hayley something or other. She's here."

"Actually I'm not a real reporter. I just write the cooking column so I really have no interest in what's going on here . . ." Hayley interjected.

"Shut up!" Shane screamed, getting more volatile and spooked by the minute.

Danny stepped partially in front of Hayley in an attempt to shield her in case bullets started flying.

"Yeah, that's the one. She's here with some guy. They just showed up unannounced and things kind of got out of my control and now we're up in Mr. Cross's bedroom and they know he's not here . . .

"Yeah . . . Uh-huh . . . They seem to know too much, if you ask me. What should I do?" Shane listened intently as he was given instructions. He nodded his head as if the person on the other end of the phone could see him. "Okay. I'll take them down there until you get here."

He ended the call and stuffed the phone back into his pants pocket.

Then he waved the gun at Hayley and Danny. "Come on. Let's go."

"Where are you taking us?" Danny wanted to know.

"The basement," Shane said weakly, a bundle of nerves.

"Why?" Hayley asked, terrified.

"Because that's what I was told to do! Now shut up and go!"

Hayley and Danny, their hands still in the air, slowly headed down the stairs as if they were on a death march, in total silence.

Hayley had seen enough movies and read enough books to know this couldn't possibly end well.

She glanced at Danny, who seemed to be in a state of denial, like he couldn't comprehend this was actually happening.

They reached the foyer and Shane ordered Danny to open the door to the basement, and then he prompted them to descend down the steps.

They hesitated for a moment, but Shane pointed the gun directly at Hayley's head, and they both obediently turned and trudged down the wooden steps into total darkness.

There was a musty, dank smell as they reached the bottom.

Shane turned on a light, illuminating a water heater and some storage boxes and not much else.

"Over there," Shane ordered.

They were herded to the far corner of the basement, which was cold and damp and quiet except for the sound of a squeaky mouse rushing away.

Shane pulled on another chain hanging from the ceiling and a bright light snapped on, blinding them momentarily.

When their eyes were able to adjust, they saw a

half-bricked-up wall that someone was working on but wasn't finished yet.

There were tools and buckets of cement on the floor.

Just inside the makeshift wall Hayley spotted something.

Was it a pile of beams that were going to be used to support the wall?

Or was it . . . ?

Hayley screamed.

It was a body.

A dead body.

Shane jumped back, startled.

Danny seized the opportunity to make a move.

He lunged at Shane, who stumbled back and pulled the trigger.

The gun went off.

A bullet whizzed past Danny's head, missing him by a mere inch or two.

It was enough for him to abort his plan to try to disarm Shane.

Hayley was still staring at the dead body.

She could now see the face.

It was turned in her direction.

A pale, drawn face.

But she recognized it.

She had seen it on the back of countless book jackets.

It was Norman Cross. "He's dead," she gasped, before turning toward Shane, her eyes boring into him. "You killed him!"

Shane shook his head vehemently. "No! How could you say that? I worshipped the man. I idolized him. I could never do him any harm. He was my friend. My mentor. I was devastated when he died."

"Well, if you didn't kill him, then who did?" Hayley demanded to know.

"Nobody," Shane said, tears filling his eyes. "He died of a heart attack."

"That's a load of crap! You're obviously bricking up his body down here in the basement so nobody finds him. Why cover up his death if it wasn't murder?" Danny shouted angrily, shaking off his fear.

He was obviously tired of being ordered about by this pesky, irrational punk.

"It wasn't my idea," Shane said ominously.

Chapter 32

They heard a door slam and shoes clicking across the hardwood floors upstairs.

Shane kept his eyes trained on Hayley and Danny, pointing the gun at them with a shaky right hand while wiping his nose with the sleeve on his left forearm.

The door to the basement flew open and the high-heeled shoes clattered down the steps into the basement until the person appeared out of the darkness into the light.

"Crystal Collier," Hayley hissed in a contemptible whisper.

She was still wearing that sharp, expensive business suit that Hayley could never afford with a matching clutch bag hanging from a strap over her right shoulder.

"They know, Crystal! They know everything!" Shane wailed, panic-stricken, gesticulating his hands wildly while holding the gun.

Crystal ducked out of the way as Shane waved the

weapon too close to her face before she snatched it out of his hand. "Give me that, you imbecile!"

She then turned her attention to Hayley.

"You just had to come sniffing around here, didn't you, Hayley? You couldn't leave well enough alone," Crystal yelled scornfully.

"You were the one who insisted I come over to your office to discuss Aaron," Hayley said. "I never would have seen the manuscript if you weren't so paranoid."

This stopped Crystal cold.

She went over the events in her mind and groaned, wanting to kick herself.

Hayley stared at the prone, lifeless body of Norman Cross. "I know what you were planning to do now. Spanky's manuscript. You weren't going to publish it as Shane's book. You were going to say it was Norman Cross's new book! If it came out as a Norman Cross novel, you knew it was guaranteed to be an immediate moneymaker! Even the crappy stories he pounds out in his sleep end up on the *New York Times* Best Seller lists for weeks!"

"Now I see why Aaron was so attracted to you. Your keen mind and impressive deductive skills. I knew it couldn't be your looks or sense of style," Crystal sneered.

Bitch.

"But this isn't just about one lousy book. It's about so much more," Crystal said, stepping forward, gun raised, pressing the barrel right between Hayley's eyes.

Hayley shuddered but stood her ground, even

though on the inside she felt as if she was going to faint.

"What the hell is she talking about?" Danny murmured in Hayley's direction.

"Crystal was Norman Cross's lawyer, and when he died unexpectedly of a heart attack, she saw an opportunity. Power of attorney. Isn't that right, Crystal?"

Crystal kept the gun pointed at Hayley's forehead. She flinched slightly.

She knew Hayley had figured it all out.

"The plan was to pretend he was still alive. Norman Cross was a recluse anyway. He rarely ventured out of the house or accepted visitors. Crystal could forge documents transferring power of attorney to her so she had complete control of his estate. Then she could just gradually funnel his entire fortune into her own accounts. To keep the illusion alive, she knew Cross had to put out a new book, so why not steal an amateur's work and publish it under Cross's name so the public would continue to believe he was still alive and working?"

Danny piped up. "Squeaky's book?"

"Spanky," Hayley corrected him. "A naive fifteen-year-old boy could be dealt with before the new Cross novel came out. Some kind of believable accident. He'd be safely out of the way unable to alert anyone to the truth. That he was the *true* author of *The Devil's Honeymoon*. And then, after most of the estate was depleted, and all that money deposited into some kind of offshore account, a story would emerge about the reclusive author Norman Cross disappearing, never to be heard from again. It would be characteristic of him. He was an oddball, a kook, an unpredictable crackpot. No one would question it.

And whoever would ultimately buy this mansion would never suspect his skeletal remains were behind a brick wall down in the basement. When I think about it, this whole despicable, insidious plot sounds just like one of Norman Cross's own stories."

"I agree. It's a tribute to his legacy," Crystal said, proud of herself for concocting such a diabolical scheme.

"I wouldn't go that far. You're not paying tribute to anyone but yourself. You're just a soulless, greedy killer," Hayley jeered.

"Hayley, maybe it would be a good idea if you toned down the heated rhetoric. What do you say?" Danny mumbled, eyeing the gun pointed at them.

"I just have one question," Hayley said, ignoring Danny.

"What's that?" Crystal growled.

"What about Otis Pearson? What happened that night? Did he see something he shouldn't have?"

"Yes," Crystal said. "He saw a poor man have a heart attack."

Shane finally spoke up, his voice quivering, his whole body wobbly. "He . . . he was here delivering his moonshine to Mr. Cross and they always had a good laugh and usually got drunk, but on that night Mr. Cross just sort of seized up and grabbed his chest and then he collapsed. Otis told me to call an ambulance, but I called Ms. Collier first and she told me not to do anything until she got here."

"Maybe if you had, Mr. Cross would still be alive," Hayley mumbled.

"I doubt that," Crystal shouted. "The man survived on cigarettes, booze, and red meat. He was a walking time bomb."

"You had no intention of telling the world Cross was dead," Danny said, jumping in. "Why allow the estate to be settled while you watch helplessly as a bunch of literary societies and charities sucked up all the money? No, you had a better plan. Keep him alive in the figurative sense until you could bleed him dry. Am I right?"

"Yes, Danny, we've already established that," Hayley said.

"Oh," Danny said, a chastened look on his face.

"Cute but dumb," Crystal said, smiling. "He must be a tiger in the sack."

"Just like Shane, I'm guessing," Hayley said.

Crystal bristled.

"Shane wasn't ever going to be a problem. You knew you had him right where you wanted him. Under your spell. I heard from his writing teacher Judith Ann Moore he had a taste for older women. You probably also kept him on a tight leash with empty promises of guiding his future to fame and fortune as a best-selling author. The next Norman Cross."

Shane shifted from side to side, hands buried deep in his pants pockets, eyes downcast. He wasn't comfortable hearing about how Crystal had used him, but on some level he knew Hayley was speaking the truth.

"That left Otis Pearson. You couldn't just let him live to tell the world he had seen Norman Cross keel over with his own eyes," Hayley said.

"No, we couldn't. I'll never forget that pathetic, almost comical look on Otis's face when he realized we were never going to let him leave this house alive," Crystal said, laughing at the memory. "He was such a sloppy, sad drunk. He ran around in circles and then went screaming out of here, running for his life. He ended up next door in the House of Horrors trying to hide from me. But I found him easily enough, and then I clocked him over the head with a club and that was that."

"That's how he got the green gunk on the bottom of his boots!" Danny exclaimed. "From the House of Horrors!"

"Yes, Danny, I know," Hayley sighed.

"Then, with Shane's help, we drove over to the cemetery and dumped his body there for someone to find. He had been drinking. He could have tripped over a gravestone. It was meant to look like an accident."

"You could have planned that part better. It didn't take the police long to figure out he didn't die out there," Hayley said.

"*Que sera, sera*," Crystal said, almost singing. "Now you leave me no choice but to shoot you two and brick you up in the wall with poor Norman. I really hate doing this."

"How perfect. Now you know for certain I will never be a factor in your happy future with Aaron," Hayley said.

"Who's Aaron?" Shane asked, suddenly confused.

"Nobody," Crystal hissed at him, cursing herself.

"Her new boyfriend," Hayley offered. "A real man. Not a boy who can be so easily manipulated."

Shane's mouth dropped open as he turned to Crystal.

"Don't listen to her. She's just trying to get you to turn on me," Crystal said evenly. "We'll talk about it later."

"Aaron's a smart man. It won't take him long to realize you're a demented, psychotic monster," Hayley said, seething.

"Who's Aaron?" Shane demanded to know.

"Never mind, Shane!"

"I'm sure it's been your dream to marry a doctor," Hayley said.

"He's not a real doctor. He's just a vet," Danny said.

Crystal glared at Danny and then she turned to Shane. "Shoot him first."

But Shane was preoccupied with this Aaron person.

He wasn't listening.

"Shane, do as I say and shoot them already!" Crystal screamed.

Their time was up.

It was now or never.

Hayley glanced over at Norman Cross's body and cried, "He's alive! Norman is alive! I just saw his finger move!"

"What?" Crystal cried, whipping her head around in the direction of Cross's corpse.

Hayley plowed forward, and just as Crystal turned back around, Hayley head-butted her as hard as she could right in the face.

The jolt of pain from the impact was crippling.

Crystal toppled over backward, crashing into a pile of bricks and knocking them over.

Danny sprang into action, wrestling the gun away from Shane and cracking him over the head with it.

Shane went down.

Crystal, holding a hand to her head, scrambled to

her feet and, shrieking like some kind of wild animal, lunged at Danny.

He fired the gun right at Crystal's face.

Click.

Everyone froze in place, motionless as if time literally stopped.

The gun was empty.

All four of them sized up the situation.

And then Crystal stared at Shane, eyes flaring. "How many times have I told you to put bullets in the gun?"

"I . . . I guess I forgot . . ." Shane said, looking away like a guilty puppy who just peed on the floor.

"Come on, Hayley, let's get the hell out of here!" Danny yelled, grabbing her hand and leading her toward the basement stairs.

Hayley twisted around to see Crystal upending the contents of the fancy designer clutch bag she had slung over her shoulder when she arrived. Lipstick, a compact, a set of keys, and a handgun all spilled onto the floor.

Crystal bent down and scooped up the handgun.

"Danny!" Hayley cried.

They had just reached the foot of the stairs as Crystal raised the gun to shoot.

Her finger wrapped around the trigger.

Everything moved forward in slow motion.

Crystal aiming the gun at Hayley.

Shane curled up on the floor like a baby rocking back and forth trying to shut out what was happening.

Hayley watching her life flash before her eyes.

Knowing there was nothing she could do as Crystal pulled back on the trigger and a shot rang out.

And then Danny suddenly hurling himself in front

of Hayley to protect her as the bullet ripped through his shoulder and he fell back with a jolt, grabbing his arm, and then sinking to the floor.

Hayley screaming as she knelt down, horrified to see blood seeping through Danny's jacket.

And then Shane screaming "No!", unable to take any more, wresting the gun out of Crystal's hand as she ferociously scratched his face with her long, sharp, painted fingernails, trying to get the gun back in her possession before Shane punched her in the face and she fell to the floor in a crumpled heap, moaning.

As Hayley grabbed her cell phone and punched in 911, she saw Shane standing over Crystal, angrily waving her handgun around and shrieking, "I want to know right now! Who the hell is Aaron?"

He was too distracted by Crystal's betrayal to hear Hayley alert the dispatcher to their whereabouts and within less than a minute they gratefully heard sirens in the distance.

Hayley leaned down and whispered in Danny's ear, "Hang on, Danny. Help's on the way."

His face was pale and his body limp, but he managed a weak smile.

Hayley never expected much from her ex-husband.

But the last thing she thought would *ever* happen was that he would take a bullet for her.

For better or worse, Danny Powell was officially now a hero.

Chapter 33

The news of Norman Cross's death swept the nation and was the talk of the cable news channels especially given the added twist of a sordid cover-up.

Reporters invaded the town to broadcast live in front of the Cross mansion and the House of Horrors.

Despite a flurry of interview requests Sergio kept Crystal and Shane locked up in the town jail after a judge denied bail, and they were not allowed to speak to reporters. A decision echoed by their defense attorney, who preferred powdering himself with makeup and speaking for them on camera since he was a rabid attention hog.

Poor Aaron's vet practice was besieged by the press when word got out he had been dating the cold-as-ice femme fatale Crystal Collier. He was rumored to have been close to shutting his business down and fleeing town until all the hoopla died down, but Aaron was a professional, and there were way too many sick animals that needed to be nursed back to health. So he just kept his head down, focused on his job, and ignored the gaggle of reporters camped outside his office who shouted questions about Crystal every night when he walked to his car after his last appointment.

And then there was Danny.

He had spent the last two days in bed recovering at the Bar Harbor Hospital.

The bullet had just grazed his arm and his minor flesh wound was patched up pretty quickly, but Danny being Danny, he relished all the attention and drama of his injury so he chose to stay hospitalized at the doctor's invitation, just to be sure he was fully recovered, even though Danny, his doctor, and the entire hospital staff knew there wasn't a single reason he shouldn't be discharged.

Hayley stopped by the hospital for a quick visit before work, and when she walked into Danny's room, she found him sitting on the edge of the bed, fully dressed in a plaid shirt over a white T-shirt, blue jeans, and L.L. Bean work boots, his arm in a cloth sling.

He perked up at the sight of Hayley in the doorway.

"Hi, babe."

"So they're finally kicking you out?"

"Are you kidding? The nurses love me. They're devastated I'm leaving. They've been fawning all over me. Tilly told me the staff got together in the cafeteria and talked about upping my blood pressure numbers just so the doctor would keep me around a little while longer."

"You always were the life of the party, Danny."

"They gave me a little going-away shindig this morning. One of the nurses baked a cake. It was very sweet. The gesture. Not the cake. The cake was dry and chalky and I had to spit it out in the sink."

Hayley chuckled.

"I'm just waiting for them to bring my discharge papers and a wheelchair so they can escort me out. I think they're having an argument at the nurses' station as to who is going to do the honors."

"You need a ride somewhere?"

"No, I'm good. I already have a designated driver. It's nice of you to stop by, Hayley."

"Danny . . ."

"I know what you're going to say. When I saved your life down in that basement, that was the moment when you realized how much you love me and that those feelings for me are never going away, so maybe it's time we tried again. You're here to tell me I should move back in with you and the kids so we can be a real family again. And that I shouldn't answer now, but I should think about it, and when I'm ready, I should let you know what I want to do even though we both know I'm going to come back to you because we are meant to be together. Am I right?"

"Not even close."

"I figured it was worth a shot. I knew you probably wouldn't go for it. I took a bullet for you. If that didn't work, what else can I do?"

"You were very brave and gallant down in that basement, jumping in front of me to protect me like that."

"I love you, babe. That's never going to change."

"So what are you going to do now?"

"I have an option or two."

From inside the bathroom, they heard a toilet flush.

Hayley raised an eyebrow at Danny, who smiled sheepishly.

The sink ran water for a few seconds and then the door opened and Becky sashayed out, wiping her hands on her tight white blouse. "They're out of paper towels."

"Becky?" Hayley said, surprised.

Becky looked Hayley up and down and with a pout said, "Oh, it's you. What do you want?"

"I just came to check on Danny. Like strictly platonic friends do. Please don't read anything into it," Hayley said, desperate to avoid another confrontation.

"Well, that's awfully darn nice of you, Hayley. But don't you worry. My Danny is in good hands. Once I get him back to Des Moines I'm going to spoil him rotten and take care of him and make sure he doesn't have a care in the world."

Danny sat up, rubbing his stiff neck, moaning a bit for effect. "You're too good for me, sweet pea."

"I know. You're lucky to have me. And don't you ever forget it again," Becky cooed, bending over and kissing him lightly on the cheek.

"Well, I'm happy to see you two back together," Hayley said.

"Liar," Becky shot back.

"Now, Becky . . ." Danny warned.

Becky threw her hands up in the air. "It's all good. I know you're not a threat to me anymore, Hayley. My Danny has made up his mind as to who the best woman is for him. Isn't that right, Danny?"

"Absolutely. One hundred percent," Danny agreed

before winking at Hayley when Becky's back was turned to him.

"You know, I had a lot of time to think while I was behind bars and I realized that I still love Danny. It's like a virus that just won't go away," Becky said, impressed with her deep thoughts.

A virus probably wasn't the best analogy she could have come up with, but Hayley wasn't going to quibble, especially since Becky was finally taking Danny off her hands.

"I suppose my passion got the best of me. It was wrong of me to try to run your car off the road. My bad," Becky said as if attempted murder were the equivalent of an offhanded insulting remark. "But everything worked out in the end."

"Well, the kids are going to miss having you around, Danny," Hayley said.

"I'll be back," Danny assured her.

"Next month is my court date," Becky said nonchalantly as if she were only facing a small traffic infraction.

There was the strong possibility Becky would be spending the next six months to two years in the state of Maine.

Serving time.

Chapter 34

Hayley was delighted to receive an e-mail from
Liddy while she was at the office later that morning.
Liddy had embarked on one of her frequent shopping trips to New York, and while she was there she
met one of her sorority sisters for dinner, who happened to be an editor at a small publisher.

Liddy had handed off Spanky McFarland's manuscript *The Devil's Honeymoon* to her college pal. The
publishing house had a small imprint of genre titles,
horror being one of them. Given the publicity sur-
rounding the plot to steal the book and publish it as
a Norman Cross novel, Liddy's girlfriend pretty
much guaranteed her senior editor would approve its
publication.

There was a lot of work to be done on the book's
grammar and plot structure, but not an impossible
task for a seasoned book editor. Liddy had already
called Spanky at his home with the good news, and
according to his mother, he was now floating on
cloud nine.

Bruce had been moping around the office ever

since Sal splashed Danny's mug on the front page of the *Island Times* as the local hero who uncovered Crystal Collier and Shane Hardy's crafty scheme to defraud the book world and make off with a multi-million-dollar fortune, not to mention murdering beloved eccentric Otis Pearson.

Hayley's name was barely mentioned in the accompanying article, and frankly she was fine with that, preferring to eschew the spotlight for once.

Let Danny enjoy his fifteen minutes.

Bruce was thoroughly bugged by all the attention Danny was getting. He felt it was undeserved, and that Hayley was downplaying her own role in solving the high-profile case.

In fact, a part of Bruce seemed resoundingly disappointed that Danny didn't turn out to be the killer of Otis Pearson.

Hayley finally decided to call him on it that morning after a particularly long rant about Danny playing up his bullet wound for sympathy, and how Bruce just couldn't respect a guy like that.

She was bolstered by the caffeine in her coffee.

Otherwise she just might have chosen to keep her mouth shut.

"Why do you hate Danny so much, Bruce? What has he ever done to you?"

"I don't hate him. How can you hate a guy who is so clearly inferior to you in every possible way?"

"Come on, Bruce. You hate him."

"Maybe a little bit. But it's only because I know how he screwed you over for years and disappointed you and the kids, and was not a very reliable husband or father . . ."

"That all may be true. But why do *you* care?"

This caught Bruce off guard.

He hadn't expected her to ask him that.

"I . . . I . . . well . . . I mean . . ." Bruce sputtered, frantic to come up with something, *anything* to say.

Hayley sat back in her office chair and folded her arms. "I'm waiting for an answer."

"If you must know . . . Okay, I'm just going to come right out with it . . ."

The door to the office opened and the strong, gusty winds brought in a few orange and brown fall leaves.

Aaron stepped inside. "Is this a bad time?"

He was bundled up in a heavy coat and his cheeks were red from the cold air outside.

"No, not at all. How can we help you, Aaron?" Hayley asked, smiling.

Bruce cleared his throat and grabbed the pot of coffee off Hayley's desk to pour himself a cup and try to compose himself.

"I was hoping to have a word with you," Aaron said before glancing at Bruce.

"I'll be in my office," Bruce said, getting the hint and turning to leave.

"No. We'll go outside," Hayley said. "It's time for my break and I need some fresh air."

Bruce nodded as he poured coffee into his mug.

It almost overflowed in his cup as he stared at Aaron before he caught himself.

Hayley grabbed her coat and followed Aaron outside.

They walked around the side of the building for some privacy.

"Is everything all right?" Hayley asked.

"Yes. I mean, aside from the TV trucks parked

outside my home and office, but I can't imagine that's going to last much longer. I just came by to thank you."

"Me? For what?"

"Well, I guess for exposing Crystal for who she really is."

"I'm so sorry, Aaron."

"Sorry? For what? You saved me a lot of time figuring it out for myself."

Hayley chuckled but then stopped herself. "I don't mean to laugh."

"They say laughter is the best medicine. And I guess I'm going to need to laugh a lot to get over this one. You know, I was really dumbfounded when all this came out. I actually thought I had pretty good taste in women," Aaron said, shaking his head before looking at Hayley. "Given my past track record."

Hayley patted his hand. "Don't beat yourself up. We all make mistakes. Believe it or not, I've made a few myself."

"Was I a mistake?"

"Of course not, Aaron."

They looked at each other a moment.

Neither was sure what to say.

Finally, Aaron laughed. "I had a dream last night that you unmasked Crystal as a thief and a murderer just so you could clear the way to get back with me."

Hayley burst out laughing.

"I know. Pretty ridiculous, right?"

"Yes."

"I mean you're done. You've moved on," Aaron said with a straight face as he gazed at Hayley. "There's no chance you would ever want to try again."

He wasn't talking about his dream anymore.

He was speaking directly to her.

Filled with nerves and anticipation.

Hayley took a deep breath and shook her head. "No, Aaron."

And she meant it.

Aaron snapped back to his lighthearted, jocular self as if nothing had happened and said, "Such a crazy dream. I better get to the office. Wish me luck with the press jackals."

"Good luck."

He jogged off to his car.

Hayley walked back inside the office, grateful for the warmth that greeted her, and sat back down at her desk.

Bruce hadn't moved very far.

He had probably been watching them from the window.

"Now, what were we talking about, Bruce?"

"I was going to say . . ."

He stopped himself and then changed tactics.

"Would you like to join me for dinner tonight? There's something I'd like to discuss with you . . ."

"Not tonight, Bruce. My kids are a little sad because their father left town today, and I really need to be with them."

"I understand," Bruce said before quietly retreating to his office.

There seemed to be a lot of men swirling around her life lately.

Danny Powell.

Aaron Palmer.

Bruce Linney.

But Hayley was truly quite happy and content being alone for now.

She had said it out loud and she meant it.

Especially when her kids needed her.

Being a mother would always come first.

No matter what.

Island Food & Spirits
by
Hayley Powell

October is my favorite month during the fall season, mostly because I love Halloween and the foliage is at its most stunning. However, this year, I have to admit, I'm ready to finally move on into November and then the colder months. October has been one wild ride for my family, and I am ready to settle into the slower pace of a desolate, quiet, slow-paced Bar Harbor winter.

I can't believe I'm saying this, but although I won't miss the drama we all lived through this past month, I will surprisingly miss my ex-husband. I know, I know. I've spent endless columns arguing the reasons why it's best we're not married anymore, but even his biggest detractors (I'm talking to you, Mona!) have to acknowledge his good points. Plus, my kids adore him and they miss him already. At least their plans to visit him during their school vacations will give them something to look forward to in the spring.

Before Danny left town, our family knew we had one more loose end to tie up and that was to give dear old Uncle Otis some sort of proper good-bye. Since Otis was definitely not a church-going man, we wanted to come up with something that would be a little more meaningful for him.

His ex-wife, Tori, suggested hiking up Dorr Mountain where we could have a small service at the top surrounded by the lush beauty of Acadia National Park. Otis loved climbing to the top of Dorr when he was young, mostly because he could smoke some weed without the threat of being spotted by his parents or a policeman.

I quickly nixed that idea because Otis hadn't hiked a trail in years. Plus, Tori was, in her own words, "barely able to walk and in failing health." Granted, some believe she embellishes her ailments in order to garner sympathy and keep her government assistance checks coming in, but that's just rumor. I, of course, don't think that, Tori! I know you read this column every day! But needless to say I was not going to risk going all the way up there only to have to call the park rangers to come and carry her down off the top of the mountain on a gurney if her back decided to go out or her legs lost feeling or she suffered an asthma attack. Also, judging by the list of Otis's aging friends, I thought the idea of a vigorous hike up a giant mountain would result in a lot of no-shows.

Finally, we agreed that we would all drive up to the top of Cadillac Mountain for his official send-off. Everyone could mercifully travel by car! We also knew this was the perfect place for a memorial service since it overlooked the scenic island Otis was born on, lived on, and unfortunately, died on a little too soon.

As the last car pulled into the parking lot of the mountain's outlook and all the mourners joined us for the impromptu ceremony, I was amazed by the size of the crowd. Apparently Uncle Otis was liked by more people then I ever knew.

Danny being Danny, and completely in his element in front of a large crowd, began a raucous send-off by telling some wildly entertaining stories about Uncle Otis's adventures from when he was a hell-raising teen to his days operating below the radar of the law with his successful moonshine business. The crowd roared with laughter. Danny had them in the palm of his hand. I swear

Danny could charm a rattlesnake, and for another forty grand, I bet he would actually try.

Once Danny finished, one mourner after another stepped forward with a funny anecdote about Uncle Otis. Everyone loosened right up and laughed heartily. I was so surprised by the love for this man. I always assumed he was a bit of a loner and kept to himself.

By the twelfth Otis story, I was starting to shiver because the breeze up on the mountain was picking up and a cold chill was in the air.

I turned to my friend Liddy, who was standing to my left, and asked, "If this doesn't end soon, I'm going to freeze to death!"

Mona, who was to Liddy's left, tipped up a clear glass bottle, which looked like it was filled with water, and chugged half of it down. Mona let out a moan and shook her head. "Try some of this! It'll warm you up real good!"

She handed me the bottle. That's when it struck me that she hadn't been drinking water! This was Otis's moonshine! I glanced around at the crowd and it appeared as if everybody was enjoying their own bottle of Otis's moonshine! No wonder everybody was laughing so hard at the stories about Uncle Otis!

It didn't take Jessica Fletcher to solve the mystery of who was behind this. It had to be Danny! He was always up for a good time, and any situation was ripe for a party, so he had brought bottles of Uncle Otis's coveted moonshine and passed them out like party favors.

After the last story, Danny called for a toast. He walked to the edge of some rocks on the top of the mountain, and had everyone gather behind him while he uncapped the urn that contained Uncle Otis's ashes and held it high in the air. Everyone else raised their bottles up as Danny made his heartwarming toast to Otis's colorful life.

I stood back from the crowd, watching and shaking my head, knowing full well that if Uncle Otis was looking down upon his nephew right now as he entertained this crowd and generously shared Otis's precious moonshine, the poor man would be rolling over in his grave. Well, if he was actually in one and not in the urn Danny was holding over his head. The point is, Otis would be spitting nails over the fact that all of these people were drinking his secret moonshine stash for free. Otis never would have stood for it if he were alive!

Once Danny finished his toast, he dramatically shook out his uncle's ashes over the side of the mountain as everyone began to take a drink from the moonshine bottles.

Unfortunately, there was a sudden huge gust of wind, and if by magic, the ashes lifted up in the air in a giant cloud and in one big whoosh they blew back and landed all over everyone at the memorial. A hush went over the crowd, and then all at once, everyone went wild screaming, spitting out their drink, trying to dust themselves off, jumping up and down, and then running toward their cars, jumping in and speeding off down the mountain. Most likely to go home and shower poor old Uncle Otis off their faces and clothes.

Danny was beside himself, covered in ashes, in a state of shock. All I could do was laugh. I swear that stiff wind was Uncle Otis voicing his displeasure over all of the free booze his nephew had handed out. I bundled Danny in the car and promised to warm him up with a big bowl of my pumpkin chili soup that I had made in the Crock-Pot before I left, and then we drove back down the mountain.

Good-bye, Uncle Otis! You will always be in our hearts. But hopefully not on our heads. It took three showers to get all the ashes out of Danny's hair.

Easy Pumpkin Chili in the Crock-Pot

Ingredients
1 tablespoon olive oil
1 pound ground beef
1 onion chopped
2 14-ounce cans diced tomatoes
2 cups fresh pumpkin
1 15-ounce can chili beans
1 15-ounce can black beans
3 tablespoons brown sugar
1 tablespoon pumpkin spice
1 tablespoon chili powder
Feel free to spice this up to your taste.

Heat the tablespoon of olive oil in a pan on the stove on medium heat; add your ground beef chopping it up with a spoon and cook until brown.

Add the ground beef and all the ingredients to the Crock-Pot, stirring to combine all of the ingredients.

Set on low heat and cook for 6 hours.

I like to eat my bowl of chili with a big slice of buttered cornbread. It's so darn good on a chilly evening.

Also there is nothing like having a chilled beer with my chili so I suggest you head out to your favorite grocery store and pick up the special pumpkin ale brews that many sell during the fall season (or look up businesses online that sell them in your area). My choice as an accompaniment to my chili is Shock Top Pumpkin Wheat ale and the best part is it comes in a six-pack!

Happy Halloween!

Index of Recipes

Turn the page for a sneak peek at

Death of a Lobster Lover

Coming Soon!

Chapter 1

Crunch, crunch, crunch.

"Mona Barnes, please tell me you are not eating food in my car!" Liddy barked, eyeing her suspiciously through the rear view mirror of her brand spanking new black Mercedes E Class Sedan.

"Nope," Mona said from the backseat, waiting for Liddy to avert her eyes back to the road before shoving her hand into the crinkled bag of Lay's Cheddar and Sour Cream potato chips again that was sitting in her lap, and extracting a generous handful of chips.

She quickly shoved them into her mouth.

Crunch, crunch, crunch.

"Mona!"

"What?" Mona sighed, swallowing and then licking her greasy fingertips.

"You just lied to my face!"

"No, I lied to the back of your head."

"It's a figure of speech! The point is you lied! You are clearly snacking back there and probably getting crumbs all over my new leather upholstery!"

"You were the one who insisted we drive in your new car," Mona said, crumpling the now empty bag of chips and tossing the trash in the empty seat next to her.

"That's because Hayley's car wouldn't have made the two hour trip and the only alternative was all of us squeezing into the front of your dilapidated old wreck of a truck!"

Hayley, who was wearing earbuds and listening to an audio book version of a Jo Nesbo crime thriller on her smartphone, yanked the buds out of her ear and swiveled around in the passenger's seat to address her BFFs. "What kind of girls' weekend are we going to have if you two are fighting the whole time?"

"I had one request, just one request before agreeing to drive us, and that was no eating in my new car. So what does Mona do? She scarfs down a bag of chips even before we've crossed the Trenton Bridge and left the island!"

"Well, you were the one who said we couldn't stop at McDonald's on the way. I was afraid I'd starve!" Mona growled.

"I said no fast food. I'm totally open to a quaint, tasteful little side of the road restaurant," Liddy huffed.

"There are no quaint, tasteful little side of the road restaurants on the way to Calais, Liddy," Hayley said, smiling.

"I rest my case," Mona said before reaching into the pocket of her gray sweatshirt and pulling out a Snickers bar, which she noisily unwrapped.

Liddy's blood boiled as she whipped her head around to glare at Mona, whose lips were smudged with chocolate as she chewed on a generous hunk of the candy bar.

"Liddy!" Hayley yelled. "Watch out!"

The Mercedes swerved back across the yellow line as Liddy jerked the wheel to the right narrowly missing a blue Ford truck approaching fast from the opposite direction. The driver pressed angrily on the horn.

"Can you *please* pay attention? I'd like to live long enough to at least see Salmon Cove," Hayley said, exhaling a sigh of relief now that the car was back to moving in a forward straight line.

Salmon Cove, Maine was a small remote fishing village located in the farthest reaches of Down East Maine near the town of Calais. When the three of them had initially discussed going on a weekend get-away during Bar Harbor's busiest time of year, in mid-July, the last place on their minds was Salmon Cove. Liddy pushed hard for them to go to Martha's Vineyard, but that was a bit pricey for her more frugal friends. Hayley's suggestion of going on a shopping trip to Portland was met with bored yawns. They already did that three or four times a year.

Finally, it was Mona who came up with Salmon Cove. She had gone there practically every summer when she was a kid. Her family owned a cabin in the woods near the scenic waterfront. The family would go fishing and swimming and play games for two whole weeks. Mona even learned her lobstering skills from a local boy whose family had a boat and a small business nearby. By the time she graduated from high school, Mona was ready to set up her own shop in Bar Harbor. Mona's Uncle Cecil still owned the cabin. Mona's father sold it to his brother after suffering a stroke. Traveling to Salmon Cove wasn't as easy as it had been for the family so they were happy to get rid of it. Mona hadn't been back since.

Mona had recently heard through relatives that her Uncle Cecil was currently visiting an old Army buddy in Arizona and so the place was just sitting there empty. She emailed Cecil, and he quickly wrote back that he was happy to offer his cabin to Mona for a few days. Hayley honestly loved the idea of not having to split a hotel room. That would leave an ample amount of spending money for decadent seafood banquets and plenty of strong cocktails. Liddy wasn't sold on the idea of a weekend in the boonies and tried to bow out of the trip altogether, but then circumstances changed.

Liddy split up with her boyfriend Sonny Rivers, a local attorney.

Or they were just taking a break.

That actually was the official story from Liddy.

But according to Sonny, it was over.

He was done.

And Liddy had yet to accept that cold hard fact.

But suddenly the idea of getting out of town had much more appeal.

And Liddy jumped on board at the last minute, insisting on driving them all to Salmon Cove in her new Mercedes that she had recently purchased in Bangor, which many in town believed was her way of trying to cheer herself up.

Hayley had pulled Mona aside before they left and made her promise not to mention the break up during their vacation and Mona agreed.

That lasted about twenty minutes into the trip.

"What you need, Liddy, is to find a new boyfriend

so he can help you get that big stick out of your butt," Mona said from the backseat.

"I don't need a new boyfriend because Sonny and I have not broken up. Like I've said over and over again, we're just taking a break."

"You can say it until you're blue in the face, but nobody's going to believe you," Mona said, popping the remainder of the candy bar into her mouth and then scrunching the wrapper into her fist before stuffing it in the seat pocket in front of her. "Why do you think he dumped you, was it the age difference?"

Hayley wanted to fling open the car door and jump out.

Liddy cringed. "No, Mona. Age had nothing to do with our decision to *take a break*!"

"Come on! It's like Maggie Smith dating the kid who played Harry Potter!" Mona howled.

Liddy gripped the wheel, her knuckles white, gritting her teeth, ready to burst a blood vessel.

"Can we *please* change the subject?" Hayley begged.

Mona shrugged, and wiped the chocolate off her face with the arm of her sweatshirt.

"Go ahead and eat all the snacks you smuggled into my car, Mona. I have no problem with that."

"What changed your mind?" Mona asked, curious.

"I'm hoping even you have enough good manners not to talk with your mouth full," Liddy sniffed.

"Don't bet on it," Hayley said, turning to see Mona tearing open a package of beef jerky.

Luckily by the time they had reached Machais on Coastal Route 1 Mona had passed out and was snoring loud enough that Liddy felt the need to crank the

volume on her radio and blast 90s classics the rest of
the way to Calais.

Hayley and Liddy bopped up and down in their
seats singing along to their favorite Spice Girls song.

"*Just tell me what you want, what you really,
really want . . .*"

The cabin was just fifteen minutes outside of
Calais and when they reached the town they had to
wake Mona up from her slumber to guide them the
rest of the way. Mona was grumpy and groggy but
she managed to get them there, and when they finally pulled up to the cabin that was at the end of a
gravel road and tucked into a secluded wooded area,
Hayley and Liddy's mouths dropped open in shock.

It was a dump.

The whole structure tilted to one side as if it was
ready to collapse.

A tarp had been hastily thrown over the entire roof
undoubtedly to cover any holes where rainfall or
snow might leak inside.

There were empty beer cans littering the property.

A rusted out Volkswagen bus with no tires in the
back.

A pitiful pile of wood stacked up against a wall.

"We're here!" Mona said, jumping out of the car.
"Pop the trunk, Liddy and I'll take our bags inside."

Hayley turned to Liddy, who sat frozen in the
driver's seat of her Mercedes, unable to move. "I
know it's not the Ritz Carlton. But it's not so bad. It
has a certain charm."

Liddy didn't respond.

She just stared at the cabin as Mona, bogged
down with her duffel bag and one of Liddy's Luis
Vitton carry-ons, tried pushing her way through the

front door that was obviously jammed. After a few tries, it creaked open and she disappeared inside.

"Maybe it looks completely different inside," Hayley said brightly, trying her best to be encouraging.

She persuaded Liddy to get out of the car and to at least go inside.

They joined Mona in the cabin.

Liddy looked around. "You're right, Hayley. It's completely different. It's worse."

It wasn't that bad.

It was recently swept and there was a full bed with clean sheets in one corner and bunk beds in another corner. The tiny kitchen at least appeared clean. No dirty dishes in the sink. And there was a small refrigerator where they could store food.

But it was small.

And calling the place no frills was being generous.

"This sure brings back a lot of happy memories," Mona said, beaming.

Liddy refrained from commenting.

She just kept walking around, taking it in, and sizing it up.

She suddenly stopped and turned to Mona. "Where's the bathroom?"

"There isn't one," Mona said casually.

"What do you mean there isn't a bathroom?" Liddy asked, aghast.

"I mean there isn't one. There's an outhouse out back!"

That's when Liddy lost it.

She grabbed her Luis Vitton carry on that Mona had deposited next to the door and stormed out. "I did not sign up for a *Little House on the Prairie* weekend! We are not Laura Ingalls Wilder and her two dirt poor sisters!"

"Not you, for sure. You're more like that spoiled brat Nellie Olsen!" Mona bellowed as Liddy slammed out the door and marched back to her Mercedes.

"Hurry up! Let's go! We're checking into a hotel!" Liddy screamed from outside.

Hayley didn't want to side with Liddy and hurt Mona's feelings, but she too couldn't imagine actually using a creaky old smelly outhouse.

And she definitely couldn't imagine in that moment that using an outhouse would soon be the least of their troubles.

Connect with Us

Visit us online at
KensingtonBooks.com
to read more from your favorite authors, see books
by series, view reading group guides, and more.

Join us on social media

for sneak peeks, chances to win books and prize packs,
and to share your thoughts with other readers.

facebook.com/kensingtonpublishing
twitter.com/kensingtonbooks

Tell us what you think!

To share your thoughts, submit a review,
or sign up for our eNewsletters, please visit:
KensingtonBooks.com/TellUs.

CPSIA information can be obtained
at www.ICGtesting.com
Printed in the USA
BVHW082251070522
636317BV00004B/6

9 781496 702548